"Do you think you could do me the most enormous favor?"
Jolie asked him.

"Could you pretend? That you are? My fiancé? Just until I figure out how to get rid of my ex?"

Jay considered that. It seemed a path rife with danger. And excitement. In other words, irresistible.

"Just until he gets it," she said hastily. "And gives up. What do you think?"

He thought it was ridiculous is what he thought. So no one was more shocked than him to hear him answering her, his tone casual. "Oh, sure. Why not? Nothing like adding an accidental engagement to your résumé."

"It'll help me with the mean girls, too."

"Oh, for Pete's sake. Haven't they grown up at all?"

"Maybe *mean* is too strong."

He doubted it. As a high school boy, he hadn't known what to do about that—the constant digs the girls took at her, the put-downs. He felt he should have done more, but the girl world then—and probably now—was baffling to him.

So, it was an easy yes to help her out. Like making amends for not coming to her defense sooner.

Dear Reader,

I feel I owe a debt of immeasurable gratitude to you, the people who still choose to read, to pick up a book or an e-reader, and immerse yourselves in a world some writer, somewhere, has created to delight you.

There are so many entertainment choices! Every single distraction we could have ever imagined is now at our fingertips: social media; games; podcasts; texts; emails; movies; webinars. All of those things are vying for a very limited and valuable resource, your time.

And so I am deeply honored that out of the hundreds of choices laid out before you today, you have chosen this simple story of home and hope—of love winning—to be a part of your journey.

My wish is that Jay's and Jolie's adventures of the heart—set against the backdrop of the gorgeous wine country of the Okanagan Valley—make you laugh, and maybe cry a little, too. My wish is that their discoveries about love uplift you, give you hope and help you believe good things happen all the time.

Finally, my wish is that when you put this book down, you feel better than when you picked it up.

With love,

Cara Colter

Accidentally Engaged to the Billionaire

Cara Colter

HARLEQUIN
Romance

Recycling programs
for this product may
not exist in your area.

ISBN-13: 978-1-335-59669-7

Accidentally Engaged to the Billionaire

Harlequin Enterprises ULC
22 Adelaide St. West, 41st Floor
Toronto, Ontario M5H 4E3, Canada
www.Harlequin.com

Printed in U.S.A.

Cara Colter shares her home in beautiful British Columbia, Canada, with her husband of more than thirty years, an ancient crabby cat and several horses. She has three grown children and two grandsons.

Books by Cara Colter

Harlequin Romance

Blossom and Bliss Weddings

Second Chance Hawaiian Honeymoon
Hawaiian Nights with the Best Man

Matchmaker and the Manhattan Millionaire
His Cinderella Next Door
The Wedding Planner's Christmas Wish
Snowbound with the Prince
Bahamas Escape with the Best Man
Snowed In with the Billionaire
Winning Over the Brooding Billionaire

Visit the Author Profile page
at Harlequin.com for more titles.

This book is dedicated to all those who still find enchantment in the written word.

Praise for
Cara Colter

"Ms. Colter's writing style is one you will want to continue to read. Her descriptions place you there.... This story does have a HEA but leaves you wanting more."

—*Harlequin Junkie* on *His Convenient Royal Bride*

CHAPTER ONE

DISASTER HAD STRUCK.

Jolie Cavaletti had been back in Canada for three whole hours, and her sense of impending doom had proved entirely correct.

She stared down into the white elegant rectangular box. It appeared to be entirely filled with pale peach-colored ruffles.

"Isn't it, literally, so beautiful?" her sister, Sabrina, breathed.

Jolie was fairly certain she heard a stifled laugh from at least two of the other members of the small gathering of the bridal party. She shot a look at Sabrina's old friends from high school, Jacqui and Gillian, or Jack and Jill as Jolie liked to refer to them.

It's only a dress, Jolie told herself. *In the course of human history, a dress can hardly rate as a disaster.*

Holding out faint hope that the bridesmaid dress her sister had chosen for her might look better out of the box, she buried her hands deep into the fluffy fabric and yanked.

The dress unfolded in all its ghastly glory. It was frilly and huge, like a peach-colored tent. The ruffles were attached to a silky under sheath, with a faint pattern on it. Snakes? Who chose a bridesmaid dress with snakes on it?

Oh, wait, on closer inspection, they weren't snakes. Vines. No sense of relief accompanied that discovery.

Jolie did feel relieved, however, when she contemplated the fact her sister might be playing a joke on her. The feeling was short-lived. When she cast her sister a look, Sabrina was beaming at the dress with all the pride of a mother who had chosen the best outfit ever for her firstborn child entering kindergarten.

Jolie glanced again at Jack and Jill, who were choking back laughter. She shot them a warning glance, and they both straightened and regarded the dress solemnly.

Inwardly, she closed her eyes and sighed at how quickly one could be transported back to a place they thought they had left behind.

Her sister, by design, or by the simple human desire to form a community based on similarities, had always surrounded herself with friends who were astonishingly like her. Sabrina took after their mother, tiny, willowy, blonde, blue-eyed, bubbly.

Beth, Jack and Jill, all of them with their blond locks scraped back into identical pony-tails, seemed barely changed in the ten years that had passed since Jolie had last seen them. They were like variations on a theme: Beth shorter, Jill blonder, Jack's eyes a different shade of blue, but any of them could have passed for Sabrina's sister.

The odd man out, the one who could not have passed for Sabrina's sister, was Jolie. She took after her Italian father and was tall and curvy, had dark brown eyes, an olive complexion and masses of unruly, dark curls.

Maybe it explained, at least in part, her and her sister's lifelong prickliness with one another, a sense of being on different teams.

"Do you like it?" Sabrina asked.

"It looks, er, a little too big."

Jolie would, in that dress, walk down the aisle and stand at the altar with the rest of the bridal party, looking like Gulliver in the land of Lilliputians.

"Well," Sabrina said, accusingly, "that's what you get for being in Italy both when I chose the dresses, and when we had the fittings."

This was said as if Jolie had opted for a frivolous vacation at an inconvenient time, when in fact she lived in Italy, going there directly after high school, attending university, earning her doctorate in anthropology and never leaving.

"It will look better on," Beth, Jolie's favorite of all Sabrina's friends, said kindly. "I didn't like mine at first, either."

"You didn't?" Sabrina said, a bit of an edge to her voice. Jolie looked at her sister more closely, and saw that premarital nerves, right below the surface, were raw.

Well, why wouldn't they be? Sabrina and Troy had been married before. A wedding that Jolie had not been invited to, not that she planned to dwell on that.

It had, according to Sabrina in way of excuse for not inviting her own sister to her nuptials, been a spur-of-the-moment thing, basically held on the front steps of city hall.

Jolie, more careful in nature than her sister, did not think a spur-of-the-moment wedding was the best idea.

Though she had not felt the least bit vindicated when things did not go well. Jolie had lived far enough away from the newly married couple that she had been spared most of the details, but her mother had reported on a year of spectacular fights before the divorce. The fights, according to Mom, who spoke of them in hushed tones that did not hide her relish in the drama, had continued, unabated, after the split.

"It reminds me of your father and me," she had confided in Jolie.

A psychiatrist could have a heyday with her sister choosing the same kind of dysfunctional relationship Jolie and Sabrina had endured throughout their childhood. Her father and mother had a volatile and unpredictable relationship, punctuated with her father's finding someone new, and her mother begging him to come back.

All that ongoing angst had made Jolie try to become invisible, hiding in books and her schoolwork, which she'd excelled at. Somehow, she had hoped she could be "good enough" to repair it all, but she never had been.

She shook off these most unwelcome thoughts. She had hoped she'd spent long enough—and been far enough—away not to be dragged back into the kind of turmoil her childhood had been immersed in.

But here Sabrina was, determined to try the marriage thing all over again, convinced that if she did the wedding entirely differently this time, the result would also be different.

A part of Jolie, which she didn't even want to acknowledge existed, might have been ever so slightly put out that her sister was having a second wedding when Jolie had not even had a first.

She had come oh-so close! If things had gone according to plan, she would be married right now. Sabrina would have been *her* bridesmaid. She could have tortured her sister with unsuitable dresses. Not that she would have. She would have picked a beautiful dress for her sister. No, better, she would have let her sister pick her own dress.

Thankfully, they had not gotten as far as the selection of wedding party dresses.

Though no one knew this, not her mother or her sister, Jolie had purchased her own wedding gown, purposely not involving her family.

Because they somehow thought she was *this* horrible peach confection.

Her wedding dress, in fact, had been the opposite of the peach-colored extravaganza she now held. It had been simplicity itself. Beautifully cut floor-length white silk, sleeveless, with a deep V at the neck that had hugged all her curves—celebrated them—before flaring out just below the knee

Even though Jolie was thousands of miles—and a few months—from Anthony's betrayal, the pain suddenly felt like a fresh cut, probably brought on by exhaustive traveling, and now being thrust into bridal activities without being the bride.

How she had loved him! In hindsight she could see that she had been like a homeless puppy, delirious with joy at finally being picked, finally having a place where she would belong. Riding high on the wave of love, she had missed every sign that Anthony might not be quite as enthused, that her outpouring of devotion was not being reciprocated.

Her breakup was three months ago, her wedding would have been in early June, if Anthony—the man she had loved so thoroughly and unconditionally, who she had planned to have children with and build a life with—had not betrayed her.

With another woman.

Something else a psychiatrist would no doubt have a heyday with given the fact she had grown up with her father's indiscretions.

And so Jolie found herself single and determined not to be sad about it. To see it as not a near miss, but an opportunity.

To refocus on her career.

To celebrate independence.

To *never* be one of those women who begged to come first. Jolie's name on her birth certificate was Jolie, not Jolene, but she had not a single doubt her mother had named her after that song.

And also she never wanted to be, again, one of those women who *yearned*, not so much for a fairy-tale ending, as for a companion to deeply share the simple moments in life with.

Coffee in the morning.

A private joke. Maybe even a laugh over a dress like this one.

A look across the table.

Someday, children, running joyous and barefoot through a mountain meadow on holiday in the Italian Alps.

Jolie tried to shake off her sudden sensation of acute distress. She made herself take a deep breath and focus on the here and now at her sister's destination wedding.

The bridal party—Jolie, Sabrina and Sabrina's other three bridesmaids—were currently having a little pre–big day preview of the facilities, which had led to this tête-à-tête in the extremely posh ballroom of a mind-blowingly upscale winery in Naramata, deep in the heart of British Columbia's Okanagan Valley.

Jolie was all too aware she was in possession of the world's ugliest dress, and that it was somehow woven into the fabric of her sister's hopes and dreams.

Unlike Jolie, sworn off love forever, Sabrina was braver. Her sister still had hopes and dreams! She was going to give love another chance.

Which kind of added up for Jolie to *Suck it up, buttercup.*

She calculated in her head. It was Wednesday already in Italy, which made it Tuesday evening

here. The wedding was Saturday. She only had to
get through a few days.

Anybody could do anything for a couple of
days. In the course of human history, it was nothing.

"I think I'll go try it on," Jolie announced.

"Yes, immediately!" Sabrina ordered, flushed
with excitement that Jolie could see the unfor-
tunate potential for hysteria in. "You're the only
one who hasn't tried on your dress."

Reluctant to actually wear the dress, but eager
to get away from her sister and the bridal party,
Jolie gathered up the box.

She went into a nearby washroom—as posh
as the ballroom—and entered one of the oversize stalls. She stripped down to her underwear,
dropped her clothes onto the floor and pulled the
dress over her head. It settled around her with a
whoosh and a rustle.

She opened the door of the stall and stepped
out, resigned to look at it in the full-length mirror that she was quite sorry had been provided.

It was as every bit as horrible as she had thought
it would be, a fairy-tale dress gone terribly wrong,
with too much volume, too many ruffles and way
too many snakes. *Vines.*

A lesson in fairy tales, really.

The bridesmaid dress made Jolie feel like a

paper-flower-festooned float in a parade welcoming the *carnevale* season to Italy.

Her sensible bra, chosen for comfort while traveling, did not go with the off-the-shoulder design of the dress, and in one last attempt to save something, she slipped it off and let it fall to the polished marble floor.

No improvement.

She fought the urge to burst into tears. She told herself the sudden desire to cry was not related to her own broken dreams.

It was because she had been home less than a few hours, and already she was *that* person all over again. Too big. Too awkward. Too *everything* to ever fit in here.

The exact kind of person a beloved fiancé— the man she would have trusted with her very life—had stepped out on.

A tear did escape then, and she brushed it away impatiently with her fist. She was just experiencing jet lag and it wasn't exactly home, she told herself firmly. Even though she was back in Canada for the first time since she had graduated from high school, Jolie was about a million miles from the Toronto neighborhood where she had grown up.

Her scholarly side insisted on pointing out it was two thousand eight hundred and seventy-nine miles, not a million.

It was that kind of thinking that had branded her a geek in all those painful growing up years. She had skipped ahead grades, and so she had always been the youngest—and most left out—in her school days. Her senior year—shared with her sister, Sabrina, two years her senior—had been the worst.

In fact, it may have been the most painful year of all.

Not counting this one.

See? Jolie could feel all the old insecurities brewing briskly right below the surface. Who wouldn't have their insecurities bubble to the surface in a dress this unflattering?

Privately, Jolie thought maybe since it was a second marriage—albeit to the same man—Sabrina could have toned it down a bit. But toned down was not Sabrina under any circumstances, which was probably why she was so eager to have a redo of the vows spoken on the city hall steps.

And really, all Jolie wanted was her sister's love of Troy to end in happiness. One of them should have a love like that!

And a more perfect location than this one would be hard to imagine, and that was from someone who had spent plenty of time in the wine country of Tuscany.

Taking a deep breath, reminding herself of her devotion to someone in the family getting their happy ending, Jolie picked as much of the dress as she could off the floor and headed back to the bridal party and braced herself for Jack and Jill's snickers, Beth's kindly pity, and her sister's enthusiasm.

But even her sister was not able to delude herself about the dress.

As she watched Jolie make her way across the ballroom to the little cluster of the bridal party at one end of it, her mouth opened. And then her forehead crinkled. And then she burst into tears, and wailed. "It looks as if it has snakes on it!"

CHAPTER TWO

JOLIE WAS UNCOMFORTABLY aware of the sudden silence that followed her sister's observation, and of the four sets of blue eyes regarding her critically.

"No, no," Beth finally said soothingly, "they don't look at all like snakes. Definitely vines."

"Even Chantelle can't fix that," Jack decided to weigh in.

"Chantelle?" Jolie asked baffled, noticing how the mention of the name deepened her sister's distress.

Jill rolled her eyes. "Only the most well-known photographer in the fashion world."

Jolie recalled it—vaguely—now. Sabrina had gushed in an email that her soon-to-be husband had some kind of connection to the famous Chantelle—one name was enough, apparently—and that she had agreed to do the wedding photography. When she *never* did weddings.

"You are literally going to ruin everything," Sabrina said to Jolie.

"I didn't pick the dress!"

"You didn't leave me time to fix it, either. Why couldn't you have come a week earlier, like I asked?"

After traveling halfway around the world to be here for her sister, it would be so easy to be offended, but Jolie recognized, again, that hysteria just below the surface.

"Sabrina, I have a job," Jolie said, striving for a reasonable tone. "I can't just put everything on hold because—"

"Oh! The all-important doctor!"

Jolie flinched that her accomplishment—a doctorate in anthropology—was being seen in this light, as if she was a big shot, flaunting her successes.

"And why would you put everything on hold," Sabrina continued, "for your sister who is marrying the same man again? You probably think it's doomed to failure. You're probably still mad that I didn't invite you the first time."

Jolie was aware vehement denials were only going to feed the fire Sabrina was stoking, and that there was a tiny kernel of truth in each of those accusations. They might hardly ever— make that never—see eye to eye, but sisters still knew things about each other.

"I can fix the dress," Beth said gently, as if any of this had anything to do with the dress. "Look!"

She got behind Jolie and pulled in several inches of excess fabric. Jolie felt the dress tightening around her.

Sabrina regarded her hopefully for a moment, then her whole face crumpled, and she wailed and ran from the room.

Jack and Jill scurried after her, sending Jolie accusing looks over their shoulders.

Beth let go of the dress. "She's just tired," she said, trailing out after her friends.

This to the woman who had left Rome over twenty-four hours ago, and been traveling ever since.

A waiter, very formal in a white shirt and black pants, came in with a tray of wineglasses. He looked around at the empty room, but did not allow the smallest flicker of surprise to cross his deliberately bland face.

"Wine?" he asked her smoothly. "I have our award-winning Hidden Valley prosecco or I have one glass of bubbly juice here, if you'd prefer?"

Bubbly juice? Jolie could not imagine any of those women choosing juice. Was it a dig at her? That drunken prom night?

Of course it wasn't. That was ten years ago. She was being overly sensitive.

"Yes, to the prosecco."

He slid a look at the dress. "Take two," he suggested.

"Thank you. I will."

The waiter glanced around the empty room, "The deck is lovely at this time of the evening."

She took his suggestion, and let the dress trail along the floor since her hands were full. She moved outside. Indeed, the deck was lovely.

Relax, Jolie ordered herself. She had to look at the events that had just unfolded lightly, through the lens of human history, even.

The dress and her sister's snippiness were hardly disasters. Didn't family frictions always surface when a little stress was added to the mix?

She settled in a lounge chair, the dress surging up and around her as though it intended to swallow her. She set down one of the glasses on a table beside the chair, took a deep breath, moved a wayward ruffle away from her face and then enjoyed a long greedy drink of the prosecco.

Ahh.

From her place on the deck, she made herself focus on the good things. Her mother was not here yet to weigh in on the dress, or anything else for that matter.

And her father was not here yet, either, bringing the more inevitable friction.

Weddings, rather than being fairy-tale events, came with plenty of tension. Strain on broken vessels—which her family could certainly be considered—was usually not a good thing.

"Here's to not having a wedding of my own," Jolie said, raising her wineglass to the glory of the evening light. She lifted her face to the last of the sun. The heat of the scorching July day was waning.

Jolie took another deep breath, and another sip of the prosecco. Well, maybe more like a gulp. She made herself focus on her surroundings rather than the troubling intricacies of her family.

The view was panoramic with lush hills, grape vines, copses of conifers and deciduous trees, a verdant green lawn stretching all the way down to the sparkling waters of a lake. Canoes bobbed gently, tied to the dock. The air had a faintly golden, sparkly quality, and a luscious sun-on-pine scent to it.

The patio was located off the ballroom and just to the side of the main entrance of the lodge. She imagined the beautiful doors thrown open for big events, people flowing seamlessly between the outside and the inside, laughter and music riding on the night air.

The main building of the Hidden Valley Winery was a sweeping, single-story log structure, at least a hundred years old and lovingly preserved. The manicured grounds only hinted at an interior that was posh beyond belief, the Swarovski crystal chandeliers and Turkish rugs inside the lobby in sharp and delightful contrast to the more rustic elements.

Jolie, to her everlasting gratitude, especially now, had found on her arrival that she had been assigned her own cabin.

I hope you don't mind, Sabrina had said. *Most of us are staying in the main lodge, but there aren't enough rooms.*

Even though Jolie was aware of already being cast on the outside of her sister's circle, she found she didn't mind at all. Especially now that she was pretty sure the tone for the wedding had been set.

Seeing her sister, with all that crowd of high school girls in the background, Jolie realized how invested she was in giving a different impression, showing them she was not that same geeky, gauche girl they might remember from their senior year.

If they remembered her at all.

A sound drifted on the summer air. Laughter. It would be unkind to think of it as cackling. Jolie recognized her sister's girlish shriek. So, Sabrina had returned to good spirits after she had dumped Jolie.

It made Jolie even more annoyed that her re-introduction to her sister's clique had gone so off the rails.

She'd barely finished exploring her little cabin

when she'd been summoned. The cabin was one of a dozen or so structures scattered through the woods that surrounded the lodge. It was completely self-contained and an absolute delight, the same mix of posh and rustic that made the lodge so charming.

But the dress reveal had been called practically before she set down her bag. Her makeup had long since given out, and her hair had gone wild. Her outfit—that she had spent way too much on in anticipation of that very moment—was travel rumpled and stained from holding her exhausted seat partner's baby for half the journey.

So, even though it meant keeping the others waiting, Jolie showered and clipped her wild abundance of dark curls, holding them back to the nape of her neck. Taming the hair was something she was much better at now than she had been in high school. She had put on a dash of makeup, pleased she didn't need much as her work, which was mostly outdoors, gave her a healthy glow. Then she had carefully chosen a skirt that showed off the length of her sunbrowned legs, and a crisp white top that was casual in the way only truly expensive designer clothing could be.

She had been annoyed at herself for being nervous when she stepped out of the cabin toward the people she had not seen for ten years.

Cavaletti, she had told herself sternly, *you are not a gladiator going into the games.*

The thought filled her with longing for the research her team was doing at the Colosseum.

And that helped her with perspective. In the course of human history, the encounter she had just survived was *not* a disaster. Not even close. And four days? Gladiators had lived below the Colosseum for years, trapped by their fates.

So the dress, technically, didn't qualify, either.

There. That was settled. In the course of human history, several days trapped at a family wedding was not even a blip on the radar. She vowed she would focus on all the good things, such as the incredible quality of the glasses of prosecco she had been given.

The first glass had disappeared rather quickly, but she *was* relaxed. Philosophical, even. She took a slower sip of the second one and worked on convincing herself that she no longer cared about being part of the *in* crowd. At twenty-six, she had lived abroad for ten years. She had a doctorate in anthropology. She was working on what she considered to be one of the most exciting projects in all of Italy, a project at the ruins of the Colosseum.

She could handle this reunion with aplomb.

Aplomb!

She wasn't the same girl in the high school

annual with a *Most Likely To*...title put under their picture.

Some of them had been ordinary: most likely to marry Mike Mitchell; most likely to run a pet store; most likely to become a doctor.

And some had been surprisingly cute and original: most likely to run away with gypsies; most likely to win the Iditarod; most likely to be a lifeguard on Bondi Beach.

And then there had been hers.

Most likely to enter religious life.

Her family had been Catholic, but not exactly what anyone would call practicing, with her parents divorced. She and Sabrina had not been inside a church since their first communion.

What had earned her that awful descriptor was that fact that Jolie had been a full two years younger than the rest of the grads. The suggestion she would join a convent and become a nun was a dig at her relative innocence. She was fairly certain it was meant without malice—someone's idea of being funny and original—and yet she could still feel the sting of it, even now, ten years later.

Which explained why she had splurged on a wardrobe that did not have one single item in it that would have been chosen by someone likely to enter religious life.

As she soaked up the serenity of the evening,

she watched as a convertible sports car, top up, a deep and sleek gray, slid into the driveway and nosed expertly into a tight parking stall.

So there it was, just a little bit behind schedule.

Jolie was pretty sure this would qualify as a one hundred percent bona fide disaster.

Because look who was getting out of that car.

As soon as she saw him, Jolie knew she should have known better than to let her guard down, to think she could outrun the embarrassing decisions that high school annual judgment on her had caused her to make.

She should have known better than to think her maturity and successes were going to make this wedding/high school reunion a breeze.

Because that man who had just gotten out of the car was the man she least wanted to see in the entire world.

Jay Fletcher.

And that was before she factored what she was wearing into the equation!

Despite the fact she had been bracing herself to spend a week with the high school crowd she had only been reluctantly accepted into because of her popular sister, at no point had Jolie prepared herself for Jay. You would think Sabrina could have mentioned he would be here.

But no, there had not been a single mention of his name.

In high school, Jay Fletcher had been the antithesis of everything Jolie Cavaletti had been.

Popular. Athletic. Sophisticated. The high school hero.

Under his picture in the high school annual? *Most likely to succeed.* And while everyone else in the grad class had only had one *most likely* under their yearbook picture, an extra accolade had been heaped on Jay. *Most likely to take the world by storm.*

If the car—sleek, rare, expensive—was any indication, he had done just that.

And Jay looked every ounce the successful man as he paused and took in his surroundings. He stretched, hands locked briefly behind his neck, and Jolie noted he still appeared to be the athlete he had once been, long-legged, broad across the shoulders, narrow at the waist and hip, some extraordinarily appealing masculine hardness in the lines of his body.

He radiated confidence, which he had never had any shortage of. But now there was a subtle masculine power about him as well. A man who had come fully into himself.

Was he beautifully dressed, or could he have made sackcloth look worthy of a *GQ* cover shoot? Really, his clothing was ordinary, just pressed khaki shorts ending in the middle of a tanned and muscled thigh, a solid-colored navy blue golf-style shirt that didn't mold his perfect build but hinted at it, which was, oddly, even more enticing. When he stretched like that, the muscles in his arms leaped appealingly.

The evening light danced in his short neatly trimmed hair, threading the light brown through with gold. It also flattered features that needed no flattery. If anything ten years had made him even more perfect.

Jay Fletcher was simply and stunningly handsome: wide brow, high cheekbones, straight, strong nose, firm, full lips, a faint cleft in a square chin.

As Jolie watched, he lifted his sunglasses. Even though she could not see the color of his eyes from here—of course she couldn't—memory conjured up the deep, cool green of them that had always made her young heart flutter.

The gaze, she reminded herself, a little desperately, that had cut her to ribbons the last time she had seen him.

Besides, she was not the young girl she had been. Not even close. In fact, she was bitter and heartbroken enough to be immune to any man.

Up to and including Jay Fletcher.

CHAPTER THREE

As JOLIE WATCHED, Jay lowered the sunglasses back over his eyes, moved to the back of his sleek, expensive vehicle, popped the trunk and threw a bag over his shoulder.

Jolie would like to claim she had barely spared him a thought over the past ten years, but that was not true. She *had* wondered if he had aged well. She *had* wondered if he was happy. She *had* wondered if he had ever spared her a thought after that last embarrassing moment together.

And yet, even as she had wondered, she had avoided asking her sister, knowing Sabrina might have guessed her pathetic interest and been cruelly amused by it.

And Jolie had certainly avoided looking Jay up online, because that would have felt as if she was indulging a secret longing for the impossible.

When she had heard his father died, her second year at university in Italy, she sent a card, but she had *wanted* so much more. To call him. To hear his voice. To be the one who soothed his pain, as if she knew things about him that others did not.

Which was silly! They had worked on a science project together and, having come to know him a little, she had deeply embarrassed herself at senior prom.

When she'd become engaged, all *that*—secret crushes and childish illusions—was left, finally, behind her. Her old life was in the rearview mirror.

But watching Jay Fletcher move toward her, his stride long and easy, Jolie knew she had been lying to herself. You didn't leave some things behind you.

And maybe it was because she was not engaged anymore that seeing Jay made her feel as if she was sixteen all over again.

Awkward.

Hopelessly out of her depth.

Like she wanted things she could not have.

She realized she had to get out of here. The jet lag. The sparkling wine. The dress. The old gang. Now Jay. It was all too much.

But then she realized, with a hint of panic, there would be no slipping away, not in this dress! She'd look like a barge heading off into the setting sun. It was too late to compose herself for the reunion she had not expected. At all.

The man Jolie Cavaletti least wanted to see

in the entire world was already halfway up the walkway. Jay came up the wide stairs that led to the entrance of the Hidden Valley Lodge.

She held her breath.

Maybe she'd be lucky and he'd just go in those wide front doors, with barely a glance toward that side deck, dismissing the woman sipping wine alone as some kind of crazy eccentric in her peach explosion.

For a moment, as impossible as it seemed with the dress screaming, *Look at me*, it actually seemed that might be how it would play out.

He glanced her way, but didn't even change his stride. Just when she thought she could breathe again, he stopped abruptly, took a half step back and stared at her. And then he lifted his sunglasses.

She'd remembered his eyes with one hundred percent accuracy, unfortunately. They were absolutely, gorgeously mesmerizing, as luminescent and as multilayered as green jade.

A smile tickled across the unfairly sensuous wideness of his lips.

It was a good thing she was well armed with cynicism, otherwise she might find his attractiveness tempting.

She'd allowed herself to give in to that particular temptation once before, she reminded herself tartly. The memory of how well that had gone should have kept her in check.

"Jolie?" he asked. "Jolie Cavaletti?"

That voice, damn him! Who had a voice like that? A movie star voice, a bit raspy, a bit tinged with laughter, a bit like fingertips touching the back of her neck.

Now what? Did she get up from her lounge chair and go over to him. Offer her hand? Say in dulcet, husky tones, *Nice to see you again, Jay. It's been a long time.*

Pretend she wasn't wearing the dress?

Instead of getting up, Jolie hunkered down deeper into the folds of her fashion catastrophe, took a fortifying gulp of prosecco—good grief, where had that second glass gone—and lifted a hand. She hoped the gesture was casual—maybe even faintly dismissive—but she feared she had only managed to look like a fainting Southern belle.

"Jay," she said.

He didn't appear to notice lack of invitation in either her tone or her feeble hand gesture. He strode right over, and looked down at her.

His scent—soap and, more subtly, mountain-air-scented aftershave—whispered across the space between them.

Don't look at his eyes, she ordered herself. *You'll turn into stone.*

But, of course, that wasn't really her worry at all. The opposite. That the light in those eyes could melt the stone she had placed around her bruised heart.

She looked at his eyes.

They were the color of a cool pond on a hot day, sparking with light like sun dancing across a calm surface.

"How are you?" he asked.

I've had better moments.

"Peachy," she said.

It was unfair how the amused upward quirk of that sexy mouth created a dimple in his cheek and made him even more breathtaking. It was unfair to notice that his hair was the exact color of a pot of melted chocolate, and that the faintest shadow darkened his cheeks and chin.

She had a completely renegade thought: she wondered what those whiskers might feel like scraping against tender skin.

Those kinds of thoughts were not permitted in a woman newly dedicated to being independent, to creating her own happiness.

She gave the prosecco an accusing look, then couldn't decide whether to take another fortifying sip or set it down. So, she did the logical thing. She did both.

Apparently oblivious to his effect on the jet-lagged, deeply embarrassed woman in front of him, he tilted his head and looked at her more deeply.

"A peach. Picked fresh off the tree."

"Well, not picked by me," she said. She hoped for an airy tone. She sounded defensive.

The upward quirk at the corner of his lip deepened, and so did the dimple. "Of course you didn't choose that dress. So not you."

Did she have to be reminded, right out of the gate, why she had had such a crush on him? He had always seemed to see in her something that everyone else missed. Jolie was engulfed with a sense of being starstruck and tongue-tied and sixteen all over again.

Cavaletti, she told herself firmly, *stop it*.

"I've seen a lot of ugly bridesmaid dresses over the years," he decided, leaning toward her and regarding her intently, "but that one might win. Are those, er, worms?"

"I thought snakes."

"Hmm. I'm pretty sure that involved an apple, not a peach."

Really? Being with a man like this made the temptations of the garden seem all the more understandable.

"And maybe a fig leaf," she replied, "which would be a considerable improvement over this dress."

She intended the remark lightly, but for a moment something scorching hot flashed in his eyes, as if he imagined her unclothed in the garden.

Jolie could feel a blush heating her cheeks. She had intended the comment to be funny and sophisticated, to wipe memories of her sixteen-year-old self from his memory.

However, it had come across as risqué. She hoped the gathering darkness hid the blush from Jay. He would think she was still the innocent woman-child who once had a crush on him.

Less than two minutes with him, and she could feel an old flame leaping back to life. This was what he had always done. Made her aware of some age-old and primal longing inside of herself to explore every single thing it meant to be a woman.

Still, she admitted to herself that she enjoyed the heat in his eyes and the fact that, finally, she had managed to tempt him.

The last time they'd been together, he'd been convinced she needed his protection.

Protection from herself, her crush on him and the embarrassing proposition he had rejected that night.

Her worst memory of all time.

Jay was tired. It had been a long drive. He'd had a sense, though, of it being worth it as he had finally arrived at Hidden Valley Winery. The sun was setting and it drenched the land in light, almost mystical in its beauty.

His sense of being caught in something otherworldly had only deepened as he had gone toward the entrance of the winery.

At first, in the fading light, he hadn't seen the woman there.

But then he had caught a glimpse of her, peripherally, and though he was not a man given to enchantments, that had been his thought. Enchantment.

He'd been shocked that it was Jolie Cavaletti. Of course, he'd known she would be here. She was the bride's sister.

But somehow he'd been unprepared for her, and especially unprepared for her turning that hideous dress into something else altogether. A fairy, sitting in gossamer folds, bathed in the golden hues of a sun already gone down.

A fairy, but as always with Jolie, there was the tantalizing contradiction, because as he'd gotten closer he'd been aware of seeing, not fairylike innocence, but a certain understated sensuality that made him aware of her as one hundred percent fully adult woman.

This had always been her contradiction. In high school, she'd been so much younger than everyone else, and trying so hard to overcome that, to be accepted. And yet, at the same time, she had remained the earnest little scientist, with big round glasses and owl eyes. He remembered her in white lab jackets, usually with some kind of stain or burn on them. The absent-minded scholar.

But then there was the contradiction: the woman's full curves, the corkscrews of curls she was never able to tame, the delicious plumpness of her bottom lip, the cinnamon scent of her.

He found himself leaning in.

Yes, it was still there, exotic and spicy, a hint of something Mediterranean.

Her remark about the fig leaf had intensified his awareness. She wasn't an off-limits kid anymore, and that felt wildly dangerous. Maybe because the drive had left him tired, he gave in to the desire to play with the danger a tiny bit.

"Why don't you surprise Sabrina?" he suggested, deadpan. "Can you imagine her face if you came down the aisle in a fig leaf?"

He saw that look in her eyes that he'd had to fight until the very last moment he had seen her, Jolie going in the door to her house, shoulders slumped, after the senior prom.

She'd turned around that night, and touched her lips with her tongue. If it had been sensual as she intended, instead of uncertain as it had presented, they might have ended up in a different place that night.

Instead, he'd had to be haunted for years, by her despondent, small voice.

Is that your final answer?

Of course, she'd been trying to be funny. It had been a question posed by a game show that had been popular at the time. Only smart people need apply. If Jolie Cavaletti had gone on it, she would have been a billionaire long before he was. But somehow, it had not come across as funny.

If she licked her lips right now, he'd be helpless.

But she didn't.

She snickered.

In some ways it was worse than the lip-lick because it reminded him of how she had been. Shy and earnest, but with something wilder and bolder brewing right beneath the surface, that dry sense of humor that he, as an adult, now associated with keen intelligence.

Which, even then, she'd had in spades, an intellectual giant who towered over kids much older than her.

"Fig leaf down the aisle," she mused, considering. And then she said, "I will, if you will."

Just like that they were laughing together. The shared laughter did the very same thing to him that it had done ten years ago.

Made every other care in the world become

nothing more than motes of dust, dissolved by the light that sparked in Jolie Cavaletti's doe dark eyes.

A waiter appeared, with two flutes of what appeared to be a sparkling wine, which would never be his first choice.

"I can't have one more drop," Jolie said. "I've got jet lag so bad it's wiping me out. I mean fig leaves really aren't something I would normally bring up."

"You don't say," he teased her.

And then she was blushing.

Blushing.

And it was as if not one day had passed since prom night and a slightly drunk sixteen-year-old Jolie Cavaletti—who had not looked sixteen in a gorgeous gown, with makeup on, and her hair, for once tamed, piled on top of her head—had leaned into him and whispered a dangerously tempting proposition in his eighteen-year-old ear.

To this day he was not sure how he had managed to put her needs ahead of his own, resist her invitation and hustle her back to her house before she found somebody who would not be able to resist her considerable temptation, who would not have given her the correct final answer.

Which was no.

The waiter had two flutes and he offered one to Jay. "Sir?"

"Oh, why not?" Jay took the proffered glass,

let his bag slide off his shoulder and settled easily into the lounge chair beside her.

In the last of the day's light, with a chilled glass in his hand and night closing in around him, with Jolie's cinnamon scent tickling her nose, and the dress making her look like a fairy in a flower, he felt...not just enchantment.

Something far, far more dangerous.

A sensation of coming home.

CHAPTER FOUR

OUT OF THE corner of his eye, Jay watched Jolie fight with the temptation of the wine for a second or two.

And then with a resigned sigh, she picked it up, twirled the stem between her fingers and took a sip.

"Don't even think about the last time I was drunk with you," she warned him.

"I wouldn't," he promised, ridiculously, since he already had. "Not that you were exactly drunk. Tipsy."

Uninhibited.

"I probably should have thanked you for that night. For you know…"

She was blushing again.

He did know. Saying no. Not taking advantage of her. He was sorry she was still embarrassed about it.

"I don't know what got into me."

"I do."

"Pardon me?"

"Some of us spiked the punch."

She glared at him as if suddenly it had happened yesterday and not ten years ago. Was she going to slap him?

"And I thought it was just your good looks and charisma that were intoxicating me!"

"I thought we weren't going to think about it," he reminded her hastily.

"If it was never mentioned again, I'd be okay with that," she said.

"Deal." He paused. "Even if you are in a dress that makes one think of a peach, ripe for the picking."

She did hit him, then. A light slug on his shoulder. He liked it. He laughed. So did she, and that awkward moment—this one, and the one that had happened ten years ago—were both gone.

For now.

With a woman like her—innately sensual, both then and now, without an awareness of that—those moments would never really be gone.

And she was no longer a child. He felt the danger of her again.

"How's your family, Jay? I'm sorry about your dad."

She had sent a card. Strange that he would remember that at all through the haze of pain. There had been a hundred cards. More, maybe. It must have been the Italian postmark, or maybe it had been her words. She had shared a memory of seeing his mom and dad walking hand in hand in their Toronto neighborhood, and said she had felt the love they had.

That she had felt it and that everyone who had ever been around them had felt it.

There was no better question than *how is your family?* to diffuse his dangerous awareness of her.

Because his perfect family had become a mess that day, and they still hadn't recovered. His mother and father had had one of the greatest loves he'd ever seen.

He'd been in university when his father had been diagnosed with cancer.

He had died with stunning swiftness. Jay's mother had never recovered. Her hero was gone. It was as if his illness had betrayed her in a way she could never get over. She was simply unprepared to deal with life alone, without her soulmate.

And so Jay had been left with the terrible lesson, that love, the thing he'd grown up believing was the strongest and greatest of all forces, was also a destroyer.

His mom, to this day, lived in the family home, but she had let the flower beds go, and watched too much television, and couldn't seem to muster any interest in life.

After the death of his father, there had been no choice. He had left college and gone home to look after the family his mother, swamped by grief for his father, abandoned. One minute, he'd been involved in football and frat parties, the next he'd been trying to cook dinners and check homework, and tell his sister, Kelly, that no, she could not wear that to school.

Out of all the people who had surrounded him during those sparkling days of high school and college, only Troy, his neighbor and best friend since he was four, had remained when Jay's world had been shattered.

Always there. Showing up with pizza for the whole Fletcher crowd. Dropping by with movies and popcorn, taking the kids to the amusement park so Jay could have a break from the sudden dump of responsibility.

Of course, Jay would accept the invitation to be best man—for the second time—for the man who had been there for him, always, even as his own mother had not.

She had been like a ghost during that time, which caused a confusion of feelings: sympathy, worry, anger, resentment, powerlessness.

Mom, snap out of it. The kids need you. I need you.

But nothing he had said could snap her out of it. Love had destroyed her, and she would not allow love—not even the love of her children— to repair her.

His two brothers, Jim and Mike, thankfully, were on their career paths, and Kelly, the youngest—the one who accused him of being commitment phobic—was just out of university. She had a newly minted degree in clinical psychology and a certain frightening enthusiasm for saving the world's damaged people.

Of which she considered Jay to be one.

Was it so hard to see all that responsibility had exhausted him?

He returned to Jolie's question. How was his family? It was a complicated question. He answered it as he always did.

"Fine. Everybody's doing fine." He turned the question away from himself before she probed any further, because she was gazing at him with eyes that threatened to see things others did not. "I heard you're a doctor. Should I call you that? Dr. Cavaletti?"

"Good grief, no. As soon as people hear that, they feel compelled to unburden not so interesting medical stories and conditions on me."

"Actually, I have this lump—"

He was rewarded with another thump on his shoulder. For someone who had become so wary of all the things associated with home, he wondered why it felt kind of good to feel at home with Jolie.

* * *

Jolie was way too aware of the nearness of Jay, of the wideness of his shoulders, the hard muscle of his thigh beneath the fabric of his shorts, the long length of his legs as he stretched out comfortably on the lounge chair. His scent, mountain fresh and masculine, as intoxicating as the wine, danced on the air in the space between them.

Jolie knew she absolutely did not need another glass of prosecco, but the waiter had set it down on the table beside her and whisked away the empty glasses.

Not even one more sip, she had told herself.

But, somehow, she picked up that glass, twirled it between her fingers and lifted it to her lips almost as if she had no control over herself.

And that was the only thing she needed to remember about Jay Fletcher.

That when a woman most needed control, around a man like him, it might be as impossible to achieve as resisting one more sip of wine.

"You haven't changed a bit," Jay decided.

"Well, except, hopefully, for the dress."

"We've already established you would never pick a dress like that."

She wondered if feeling like kissing a man could simply be interpreted as gratitude for being *seen*?

"Thank you," she said simply.

"Not then, not now. The absent-minded genius. Inside-out shirts. Chemical stains on your lab jacket."

If she'd been absent-minded around him, it hadn't been because she was a scholar. She was not at all surprised by his memory of the inside-out shirt. That reflected, exactly, how he had made her feel. Inside-out. She hadn't been able to think straight around him, her normally logical brain completely scattered.

"You would have set a dress like that on fire on the Bunsen burner."

"On purpose."

They were laughing again.

"Do you love Italy?" he asked her, after a moment.

"Love. I finally found a place where I fit."

She hadn't meant to blurt *that* out. Of course, how much of fitting in had to do with being welcomed into the folds of Anthony's large and boisterous family, the kind of family she had always dreamed of?

She thought of his *nonna* always cooking, always laughing, always bouncing babies and shooing children, and giving her the one thing she'd never had, a sense of belonging.

Like this, Nonna had said, then watched Jolie approvingly as she stretched the pizza dough. That pinch on the cheek.

If she was honest, she missed all that much more than she missed Anthony.

He regarded her thoughtfully. "You didn't really fit."

"And still don't," she said with a sigh.

"It's what I liked best about you."

That took her by surprise. Until that embarrassing night of the grad prom, she was pretty sure, that she had barely been a blip on Jay's radar.

He'd liked something about her?

His lips quirked upward. "Remember that science project?"

She pretended to be thinking about it, scanning the banks of her memory for something elusive.

"We extracted DNA from a strawberry?"

He remembered that stupid experiment. What she remembered was her stomach jumping at his closeness, the scent of him filling her nose, liking his laughter, the excuses to brush against him, touch his hand with hers...

"Did we?" she asked.

"When the teacher first assigned you as my partner, I was so disappointed."

"Don't hold back," she said.

"Not because of *you*. I wanted Mitch Ryerson. I thought he was the smartest person in the class and that he could drag my sorry ass through it.

And then I found out you were the smartest person in the class. Possibly in the whole world."

"That's an exaggeration," she said.

He cocked his head at her. "How many grades had you skipped by then?"

"Two," she said, "And I don't remember you having a sorry ass."

Though she remembered his ass—and coveting it—with embarrassing clarity.

Do not blush, she ordered herself. "So, what's your connection to the wedding party?" she asked, which was so much more cosmopolitan than *what are you doing here?*

"I'm the best man."

Of course he was. Most likely to be the best man.

"I was the best man at their first wedding, too," he said, and something flitted through his eyes. "Troy and I were next-door neighbors since we were four."

"Oh, really? I don't even remember Troy in high school. I thought Sabrina said she met him at one of the neighborhood pubs."

If she had known they were such good friends she might have been better prepared for this meeting.

"He never went to our school. He went to private school. We're kind of like family, always there for each other."

Family. Always there for each other. Maybe he could send a memo to Sabrina.

"I wasn't able to get back in time," she said, which allowed her a little more dignity than *I wasn't invited. To my own sister's wedding.*

"Yeah, it seemed very, er, spontaneous. Just four of us, at city hall at high noon."

"I think Sabrina always regretted that. That she didn't have the traditional wedding. I think she wants everything to be different this time."

Everything. Especially the result.

He didn't say anything, and she felt compelled to rush into the conversational lull.

"So, what have you been doing with yourself?" she asked. And then wished she hadn't. The whole wedding party was going to be here until next Sunday morning. There would be lots of time to find out what he was doing with himself.

Or maybe not.

Maybe this would be her only opportunity to be alone with him.

Please, God.

But she was aware of the ambiguity of the prayer. *Please, God, no more opportunities to be alone with Jay Fletcher,* or *please, God, lots more opportunities to be alone with Jay Fletcher?*

"I started a little sporting goods company. It's done okay."

She couldn't resist glancing over at the car.

That was a pretty expensive bag draped over his shoulder, too. She suspected he had done quite a bit better than okay.

She frowned. Another sports car was pulling in, way too fast. The sudden screeching of tires was incongruous to the deep evening quiet settling over wine country. They both focused toward the parking lot.

This car was also a convertible, candy apple red, with the top down, spraying gravel in a show of the vehicle's great power. It flew into a parking spot, nearly careening into the car beside it. The driver did not correct the awkward angle, but shut off the car.

Jolie actually felt terror as she glimpsed, over the back headrest, the bright blond hair shining like an orb against the pitch black of the completely fallen night.

Please don't be him, she thought.

Jay Fletcher moved down one notch in the list of people she least wanted to see in the entire world as she watched the vehicle, her heart thudding in her throat.

She stared, with disbelief, as disaster struck, this time for real. Not the least debatable on the disaster scale.

She wasn't aware she had made a sound, until Jay touched her arm. "Are you okay?"

"Only if you have an invisibility cloak," she

managed to say, and then wished she hadn't, because despite her distress over Anthony's appearance, that was a particularly nerdy thing to say.

What could her ex-fiancé possibly be doing here, in a popular tourist region in Canada that was nonetheless hard to reach. It was *not* a coincidence.

She got up out of the chair, looking for an escape route. There was none. Still, she felt everything in her try to shrink, to disappear—as if that would ever be possible in this dress—as her former fiancé, Anthony Carmichael, got out of the vehicle. He didn't open the car door. He leaped over it.

In the range of chance, what were the possibilities that she would have to face the two men she wanted to see the least in the entire world in the very same instant?

And here came Anthony, charging up the steps, all that energy snapping in the very air around him.

He was stunningly handsome, but in a totally different way than Jay Fletcher was handsome. He looked like a man in those old paintings, posing, one hand tucked inside a brocade waistcoat, a certain arrogance stamped across perfect, fine features.

Stunned, Jolie realized Anthony did not look anything like his boisterous Italian relatives. He looked something like her mother. And her sister. And every other member of the wedding party.

Considering how Italy had made her feel like she fit in for practically the first time in her life, how was it she had gravitated toward him?

Another heyday for a psychiatrist!

CHAPTER FIVE

FOR A HOPEFUL moment Jolie thought that, just like the other man she had least wanted to see, Anthony's endless energy would propel him right on by her.

Of course, she was not that lucky. He stopped in his tracks when he saw her. He took her in, changed course, bearing down on her with frightening singleness of focus. Finally, he stopped. Too close. In her space.

Good grief. It looked as if he intended to take her hand, kiss it and bow. She tucked her hands behind her.

"Jo," he said. "You are like something out of my dreams. That dress!"

Having been deprived of her hand, he kissed his own fingers then flicked the kiss to the wind.

Had he always been so affected?

Of course he had. She had been so in the throes of love she had been blind to every flaw. Except the last one.

She was suddenly aware of Jay getting up from

his lounge chair and coming to stand beside her. She glanced at him, and he slid her a questioning look out of the corner of his eye. Something changed in his stance. He inserted himself, ever so subtly, between her and Anthony.

"Anthony, what are you doing here?" she stammered to her former fiancé.

Anthony, ever jealous, shot Jay an appraising look. She could sense Jay grow in stature, a quiet intake of breath, a subtle broadening of already broad shoulders. When she glanced at him again, he was returning Anthony's look with a flinty steadiness. Anthony looked away first, focusing on her with that familiar intensity.

"Your sister invited me," he said. "She knows the truth!"

Jolie registered Sabrina's betrayal like a blow. "The truth?"

"We belong together," Anthony exclaimed, switching to Italian. Anthony was an expat, like her. He'd grown up in Detroit, Michigan. He'd gone to Italy in search of roots almost forgotten by his family. He had found them, on his mother's side, and been instantly welcomed into the fold. As had she, when she started dating him.

Still, Anthony's Italian wasn't perfect, but it served him to switch languages in order to lock Jay out of the conversation.

Jay shot her a look. She felt as if her pathetic

love for this man who had betrayed her was an open book. Jay inserted himself more firmly between her and her ex-fiancé.

Jolie could probably count the impulsive things she had done in her life on one hand. The most regrettable involved the man, not in front of her, but beside her.

Maybe what happened next could have been Jay's fault, just like him spiking the punch on that long-ago night. Maybe he coaxed out her impulsiveness. Or maybe her need for self-protection trumped common sense at the moment.

More likely, it was way too much prosecco, an empty stomach and jet lag. And maybe the dress could even be thrown in for good measure.

But, whatever the reason, she stepped more closely into him, and then firmly took Jay's hand in her own.

She wasn't expecting the fit to be quite so comfortable. She wasn't expecting to feel his strength surging into her.

She wasn't expecting—given the awkward discomfort of the circumstances—to be so *aware*.

"You and I don't belong together, Anthony," she said. Her voice reflected the strength she was gaining, through osmosis, from Jay.

"We do!" Anthony insisted, still in Italian.

"We don't." She spoke English, her voice clear and certain. "This is my fiancé, Jay Fletcher."

Jolie felt Jay's shock ripple through him. She braced herself in case he dropped her hand. But instead, his grip tightened on hers. She glanced, once again, quickly, at his face. He did not look stunned at all. In fact, he smiled at her with just the right touch of possessiveness.

On the other hand, Anthony looked, unsurprisingly, completely stunned. For a blissful moment, she almost believed he would accept defeat.

But then Anthony's brow furrowed. He looked between the two of them suspiciously.

"This isn't even possible," he declared, as if he was in charge of all the possibilities in the world. "You are just trying to discourage me. It happened too fast."

He spoke English this time, to make sure they both understood him.

It had been three months since her breakup with Anthony.

"It's not fast," Jay said firmly. "Jolie and I have known each other forever. Haven't we, honey?"

Honey. Under other circumstances she would have certainly savored that sweetly old-fashioned endearment coming off his lips.

"Forever," she agreed.

For a moment, Anthony looked uncharacteristically flummoxed. But that look lasted only a moment before his customary confidence returned.

Only with Jay standing beside her, she felt as if

she was redefining confidence. Anthony's posture had something faintly off-putting about it, the posture of a man who swaggered.

Why hadn't she seen it before?

Blinded by love, that's why! A good reminder of what love did to people, especially with her hand nestled so comfortably in Jay's, as if it belonged there, as if it had always belonged there.

"You don't have a ring!" Anthony pointed out, triumphant.

"We decided we didn't want to take away from Sabrina and Troy's big event," Jolie said smoothly, shocked at how easily the lie slid off her lips. "We're going to announce our engagement after the wedding."

Anthony glared at her. He gave Jay a distinctly pugnacious look, as if he might be planning on inviting him to a duel.

In Italian, she said to him, "Please, just go. You are going to make things awkward. You'll ruin the wedding."

If the dress doesn't do it first.

"Your sister invited me," he reminded her.

She would be having a talk with Sabrina about *that.*

"She doesn't know about Jay and me As I said before, we didn't want to take away from her big day."

"I'm not leaving," he answered in Italian. "I'm winning you back."

"You can't win me back. As you can see, I've moved on. You cheated on me." She was glad that humiliating detail was revealed in Italian.

He lifted a shoulder. "I've apologized. I have promised to change. For you."

As if he was willing to put himself out, *for her.*

"It's too late," she said firmly. How could she have ever fallen for him? The thing was, despite what Jay had said about her being the smartest person in the world, she was not.

In some areas, she was downright dumb.

Needy.

Naive, even.

Look at the way she felt about the hand in hers, despite her near-miss with Anthony!

Her former fiancé looked narrowly at her, and then at Jay.

"He's not for you," he proclaimed, still in Italian. "What's he got that I haven't?"

Since they were speaking in Italian, and since Anthony was determined not to get the message, she felt as if she had no choice but to be a tiny little bit cruel.

"He's got quite a bit that you don't have," she said with a coy smile.

Anthony's mouth fell open. His whole face

reddened. And then he said huffily, "It doesn't matter what you have. It matters how you use it."

Jolie felt increasingly desperate to get her message across. That she had moved on. That it was well and truly over and that Anthony had absolutely no chance of winning her back. Ever.

Words, obviously, were not enough.

She turned into Jay.

He'd been a good sport so far.

Please don't step back, she pleaded silently as she stepped right into him.

Full contact. She could feel his heat radiating out from under his shirt. She could feel the strength of him. She could feel the hard, steady beat of his heart.

She looked up at him, looked deeply into the amazing green of his eyes, touched her lips, tentatively, with her tongue.

Then, she committed. Jolie wrapped her hands around his neck, and she drew his lips down to her own.

She kissed him.

And she kissed him hard.

As soon as her lips met his it felt as if she had been waiting for this very moment since she was sixteen.

And that it was worth a ten-year wait.

Everything else, including Anthony, faded away.

* * *

If Jay Fletcher was going to pick his top ten most unexpected moments, Jolie Cavaletti claiming his mouth with her own would certainly be up there.

Her lips were soft, and he found the invitation of them irresistible. She tasted of wine and night and the stars.

The kiss quickly moved into the number one position of his life's unexpected moments, just nudging out his other surprising encounter with Jolie, which had held the number one position for ten years.

He remembered this study in contrasts. How could someone be sweet and on fire at the very same time?

How could a kiss that was staged—a pretense—feel like the most real thing that had ever happened to him?

"He's gone," he said against her mouth, looking over her shoulder.

She broke away from him abruptly. Her lips looked puffy, and her cheeks had spots of color in them. Her eyes sparked with the fire he had tasted.

"Wow," he said softly, "you look like a princess in a fairy tale."

"It's the dress," she said, sharply. "Don't let it fool you. I don't believe in fairy tales, and I certainly don't need a prince to wake me up."

It was a rather shocking lack of gratitude given

how gamely he had played along with her ruse when her spurned lover had showed up.

Maybe she was just covering her embarrassment, or maybe she didn't want him to know that she had found that as delightfully unexpected as he had.

But she was definitely trying to cover something, looking avidly and hopefully toward the parking lot, as if she was totally focused on the *goal* of that kiss and not the unexpected treasure discovered.

"He went the other way. To check in, I assume."

She swore in Italian.

They both came from the same heavily Italian neighborhood in Toronto, but Jay was Italian on his mother's side, and she had been blue-eyed and fair, as were many of the people from Cremona where his maternal grandparents hailed from.

It seemed duplicitous not to tell Jolie, right now, that he spoke Italian. In fact he spoke it far better than her ex-friend. On the other hand, he was feeling a bit annoyed with her.

"That was kind of a déjà vu moment," he said, unkindly.

"I thought we agreed not to talk about that."

"Not talking about it doesn't make it go away. There are some things a man doesn't forget. Strawberry DNA, a pretty girl offering her lips."

She'd actually offered quite a bit more than her

lips, but her blush was already deepening, so he was pretty sure she did not have to be reminded of the details.

"I was young and stupid."

Ouch. Why did that sting?

"That's the difference, all right," he said softly. "You're all grown-up."

In fact, her lips on his had let him know just how grown-up.

That night, years ago, it had been so evident that she was the farthest thing from all grown-up.

She cast a glance at the doors of the lodge. "He went in there? Really? Like he's staying?"

"I think you've got yourself a determined fan there," he said.

"More like a stalker. How could my sister do this to me? Her and my mother met him in Italy. They couldn't stop gushing about how he was the perfect man. He's here because they don't feel I can do any better. And that's even knowing—"

She bit her lip.

He didn't say anything because he wasn't supposed to speak Italian and therefore know that pompous creep had fooled around on her.

But it said so much about how her family saw her.

Maybe how everybody had always seen her. He, himself, had seen her that way once.

Awkward. Geeky.

But then he'd worked on that science project with her.

And found out she was formidably intelligent, but also surprisingly funny, charming and original.

He'd liked her, in the hands-off sort of way that an older guy liked a too young girl. But that moment at prom she had tried to change all the rules.

Jolie had offered herself to him.

That same way, leading with those luscious lips.

And when he hadn't even fully recovered from the shock that the awkward, geeky girl was shockingly sexy, Jolie had announced, a little drunk—from punch he was suddenly ashamed that he had helped spike—that she had decided to lose her virginity that night. And she had chosen him.

He'd hustled her out of there, into his car and home—her home—as fast as he could. He'd dumped her on the doorstep with a stern lecture and watched from the car to make sure she went in the house.

Chivalrous.

He'd done the right thing, even though he knew he'd hurt her by doing it.

And now, here they were. Did you ever really outrun anything in life, or did it always catch up to you?

CHAPTER SIX

"Do YOU THINK you could do me the most enormous favor?" Jolie asked him.

"I thought I just did," Jay returned dryly. And his kindness had been repaid with a reminder he was no prince.

"Could you pretend? That you are? My fiancé? Just until I figure out how to get rid of him?"

He considered that. It seemed a path rife with danger. And excitement. In other words, irresistible.

"Just until he gets it," she said hastily. "And gives up. What do you think?"

He thought it was insane was what he thought. So no one was more shocked than him to hear him answering her, his tone casual.

"Oh, sure. Why not? Nothing like adding an accidental engagement to your résumé."

"It'll help me with the mean girls, too."

"Oh, for Pete's sake. Haven't they grown up at all?"

"Maybe *mean* is too strong."

He doubted it. As a high school boy he hadn't known what to do about that—the constant digs the girls took at her, the put-downs. He felt he should have done more, but the girl world then— and probably now—was baffling to him.

"The problem is probably mine. Dragging along old baggage from high school. I wasn't expecting to be right back *there*. Feeling like I don't quite measure up somehow."

So it was an easy yes to help her out. Like making amends for not coming to her defense sooner. For spiking the punch that night.

"You know why, don't you?" he asked her, softly, even as he warned himself, *Stay out of it. Human relations are a topic you know nothing about.*

"Why what?"

"They treat you like that?"

"I don't actually."

"You know how photocopied pictures look when the printer is running out of ink? Faded and indistinct?"

She nodded uncertainly.

"That's what they were next to you. You were more than them. Prettier. Smarter. Infinitely funnier. And they never wanted you to know. They wanted to keep you down. Like Cinderella and her ugly stepsisters."

"Oh, for heaven's sake. I told you I don't believe in fairy tales."

It was her Dr. Cavaletti tone for sure. Nonetheless, she looked pleased.

"I'll pretend to be your fiancé," he said, "but only on one condition. That you act as if you're worthy of a man who loves you deeply and unconditionally."

There, he told himself. He'd agreed to this crazy plan for one reason and one reason only. Out of pure altruism. To show Jolie Cavaletti who she really was.

But was he going to be able to handle it when she found out?

"I'll make it worth your while," she decided.

He wagged his eyebrows at her wickedly, even as something in him sighed at how thoroughly she didn't get it.

It was okay to let people help you out. You didn't have to pay them back.

"Not like that." There was that smack on his shoulder again. It was a strange thing to like. He liked it.

"Like what, then?"

"I haven't decided. Maybe my firstborn."

"You have a firstborn?"

"Of course not!"

"Oh, but the possibilities," he said. "We could

make a firstborn. That could be how you repay. The making. Not the firstborn."

"Maybe a puppy," she said.

"I don't want a puppy," he said. "My worst nightmare."

"How can a puppy be anyone's worst nightmare?"

"Do you have one?"

"No. But I'd like to someday."

"Well, I wouldn't. I've had my fill of looking after things."

He was shocked he had let that slip out.

She regarded him thoughtfully for a minute. He remembered this look, a certain intensity in it, a stripping away of anything that wasn't real.

"Did it all fall on you, after your dad died?"

He nodded, not trusting himself to speak at how quickly and clearly she had seen it.

"And yet, here you are, looking after me," she said softly.

"Temporarily," he reminded her. "You better make sure there's some fun involved."

She looked at him again, as if she saw it all. The late nights, and the two jobs, and trying to keep the house, his siblings and his mother together.

It looked as if Jolie saw the worrying. The constant worrying.

"I will," she promised.

And he wondered, again, just what he was letting himself in for.

"We have a deal," she said, and stuck out her hand, as if she planned to shake on it.

"Oh," he said, "I think we're way beyond that."

And he kissed her with deliberate lightness on her lips.

"Maybe we need to set some, er, perimeters," she said.

"Like setting up a scientific method?" he asked her dryly.

She didn't get that he was being funny. "Exactly."

"Well, he's watching us out the window of the lobby, so what's your method going to be for dealing with that?"

She took his hand. "Will you walk me to my cabin?"

"Of course," he said.

The cabin was nestled back in the trees, with a sign over the door. Jay glanced up at it.

Lovers' Retreat.

Good grief. It was his turn to blush. There was an awkward moment when he wasn't sure what to do with his new fiancée in such close proximity to that sign.

She solved it. "Thank you," she said brightly. "Good night."

And then, Jolie Cavaletti, his fiancée, stepped inside her cabin and firmly shut the door in his face.

He traced his steps back to the lodge. The lobby was clear so he stepped in to check in. The receptionist assigned him a room in the main building. From somewhere, he could hear girlish laughter from women he knew were not girls.

He wondered why Jolie wasn't in the main building. Were they that mean-spirited that they would deliberately exclude her?

The laughter suddenly came closer and Jacqui and Gillian—whom he knew Jolie hilariously referred to as Jack and Jill—burst into the lobby.

"Jay!" they shrieked together, as if it had been a long time since he saw them, when in fact they had all been at some kind of prewedding planning session three weeks ago. It had been extraordinarily boring, and he and Troy had entertained themselves by taking turns sending each other emoji faces on their phones as Sabrina rolled out the plans. Wedding music, rolled eyes; bridesmaid dresses, green nausea face; groomsmen attire, laugh-out-loud; cake, licked lips. Terribly juvenile and the only part of the evening he'd enjoyed.

Jack and Jill had taken him hostage and filled him in on Chantelle, the photographer Troy had lined up because she was his mom's best friend's daughter or something. Both of them had done bit modeling, even in high school. Ad campaigns for local shops, some catalog stuff. They had hinted in the past they would be great choices for his sporting goods line, but he had never taken the bait.

Chantelle, they had informed him, beside themselves with excitement and letting him know the opportunity he had missed, was well-known for discovering the next big name in the modeling world. They both seemed to think they were going to be that discovery, though he was not sure how many models were discovered at their age, which was the same as his, twenty-eight.

Jay was never quite sure how his friend, earthy, honest, brilliant, loyal, had ended up with Sabrina. Her inevitable entourage, alone, would have made Jay hesitate.

But Troy loved Sabrina. He'd been a mess when the marriage hadn't worked out the first time—another cautionary tale about love, really. Still, Troy's personality seemed to balance that of his more mercurial wife. And also wife-to-be.

His friend had a kind of affectionate acceptance of the oft quirky Sabrina that was enviable.

Still, the truth was if Jay did not feel as if he owed Troy big-time, he would not even be here.

Jill and Jacqui left in a flurry of giggles and wagging fingers, and Jay slid the key back over the counter. "Have you got another cabin? Something close to…ah…Lovers' Retreat?"

The receptionist consulted her bookings. "How about Heart's Refuge?"

Who came up with these names? A thirteen-year-old reading romance novels? And at the same time, he leaned into it. He wanted to believe there were refuges for bruised hearts.

"Sure," he said.

He found his way to the cabin—next to Jolie's—her lights were on, but he took his heart into the promised refuge without giving in to the temptation to go visit with her for a while. See what she was reading. And if her hair was wrapped in a towel. If she wore pajamas with kittens on them, or silk.

Being engaged to her was going to be way more complicated than he wanted.

If he let it, he decided firmly. He was doing a friend—were they even that?—a favor. Somebody maybe he owed something to, for never standing up for her, for spiking the punch that night.

It would be best, except for when they were "on" to set the perimeters as she had suggested earlier. He would avoid her entirely, except for official wedding activities.

The next morning, his perimeters were challenged almost instantly.

Because he walked into the winery restaurant for breakfast to find The Four, as he liked to call

Sabrina and her pals, clustered around a table snickering.

They looked, with their tangled hair and smudged eyes, yoga pants and T-shirts, as if they had survived a late-night pajama party that involved booze. Actually, Sabrina looked clear-eyed. The other three didn't.

When he moved closer, he could clearly see they had a pile of clothing on the table, and on top of it was a bra.

That definitely did not belong to any of them, members of the Gwyneth Paltrow lookalike club.

"Oh, my God," Jill said, "over-the-shoulder-boulder-holder."

He was stunned by his level of fury. This is what these girls had subjected Jolie to all through high school: the constant scorn, the behind-her-back snickering, the snide judgments. He reached in over Gillian's shoulder and took the bra.

"What is wrong with you?" he said to them all, and shoved the bra into his pocket. "Grow up!"

Sabrina widened her eyes at him. "Jay! I didn't know you were here."

He could tell no one had expected to see him, as fingers ran through blond locks and clothing was adjusted.

"You should give that back to me," Sabrina said. "It belongs to Jolie. She left it on the bathroom floor last night."

Making it sound as if she had been partying along with them, and maybe even been the worst of them.

They were, of course, unaware he had already seen Jolie last night.

"I know exactly who it belongs to," he said tersely.

There was silence for a moment, and then Beth said, tentatively, "But how would you know that?"

Jolie picked that moment to walk in.

In contrast to them, she looked stunning. Her dark hair was still wet from the shower, wildly curling, but clipped back. She was wearing a lemon-yellow pencil line skirt that showed off the length of her legs and a crisp white blouse that showed off the understated sensuality of her.

She had on just a hint of makeup, a smudge around her eyes that made them look soft and brown, like the doe deer he had startled off the road on the way here. She had so much natural color, unlike the ghostly four, that she did not need blush on her cheeks. She had a touch of gloss on her lips that drew his eye there.

She hesitated when she saw The Four, and Jay watched as she shrank before his eyes, hunching her shoulders ever so slightly, shoving her hands into the pockets of that skirt. She obviously suddenly felt overdressed, as if she had tried too hard. It was all in her face: the insecurity, the fear of being made fun of.

And the jackals gathered around her bra, now in his possession, made her fear justified. It made him feel so protective that Jolie had no idea who she was. And neither did The Four.

"Ew…yellow," Gillian said under her breath.

Jolie glanced down at her skirt, and smoothed a hand over it.

"I like it," he snapped. "I like it a lot."

It was their turn to shrink, eyeing him warily.

But it was exactly as he had told her last night, and that skirt made it apparent. She was full color to their faded sepia. She was a brilliant original and they were copies.

At that moment, he committed.

To showing Jolie who she really was.

Jay strode over to her, put his arms around her and kissed her full on the lips.

It filled him with the oddest yearning that this was real. That he really got to say good morning to a woman like this, in this way.

He broke off the kiss, took her hand and led her back to the circle of women. He had to tug her slightly, she was so reluctant.

He tucked his arm around her waist.

He was quite pleased that he had, from the looks on their faces, managed to completely stun The Four.

Hopefully into silence.

"Jolie and I have been in contact," he said. Just in time, he remembered she had told Anthony they would hold off on a formal announcement until after Sabrina's wedding. As tempting as it was to cut the legs out from under the mean-spirited bride, he didn't.

"We're finding we have quite a lot in common."

He had hoped somehow to build Jolie up with that. Instead, he found he hated it, that the looks on every one of those woman's faces changed, not because of Jolie, but because of his acceptance of her.

His status, no doubt, had gone up steadily in their eyes as his star had risen. He couldn't even say how tired he was of *that*, of people adjusting their opinions about him based on his financial assets.

It was infuriating that they could be so shallow and so smugly unaware of it.

Really? In this day and age, a woman's value could be decided by her choice of a relationship? By a man choosing her?

No wonder she had stayed in Italy all these years. He glanced at her. It occurred to him his rise in the North American business world, while big news with the old high school crowd, was not such big news in Europe and had probably not reached Jolie.

He was pretty sure she had no idea he was a billionaire, and he had a sudden hope of keeping it that way.

Sabrina looked between them, quickly masking how she was appraising her very accomplished sister in a new light because of the billionaire thing.

"Jolie," she said, "I've decided the bridesmaid dress is a disaster. It can't be fixed. You'll have to find another one. There's a city not far from here. Penticton. I'll text you pictures of the other dresses. The essential part is the color. It's important for the photos."

"Color essential," Jolie repeated dutifully.

"Oh, and you left your clothes on the bathroom floor last night. For some reason Jay has taken possession of your bra. Weird. But…" she cast them a sly look "…weirder things have happened."

Queen Bee, buzzing, taking control, Jay thought unkindly. He refrained from saying that a good man like his friend Troy ending up with her would end up very high on his list of those weird, unexplainable things.

A smart, bright, vibrant person like Jolie being Sabrina's sister being another of those things.

He felt more determined than ever to show Jolie—and everyone around her—who she really was.

"Take Jay with you," Sabrina said, her tone

dripping acid. "He's cranky this morning and who needs that kind of *energy*."

Completely blind, as those people so often were, to her own toxic energy.

"Yes," he said, "let's grab breakfast in town."

He couldn't wait to get away from them. He took Jolie's elbow and guided her outside. He didn't realize she'd been holding her breath until she started breathing again.

He fished her bra out of his pocket and she snatched it from him and put it in an oversize bag.

"You don't have to come dress shopping," she said.

It was true, it was not how he'd expected to spend the day. He'd thought maybe a bit of waterskiing with Troy when his friend arrived later today.

On the other hand, he hadn't expected to end up accidentally engaged, either.

There was something about the unexpected occurring in his generally well-ordered life that intrigued him, and that he was not going to say no to.

Even if it did mean spending part of a day looking for a bridesmaid dress, of all things. Though, come to think of it, maybe that was going to be the most fun he'd ever had on a shopping trip.

Because look what he was trying to accomplish and look what he had to work with.

CHAPTER SEVEN

JAY HELD OPEN the door of his car for Jolie.

"Is this part of your award-winning acting skill?" she asked. It seemed to her Jay was doing a stellar job of pretending he was her romantic interest.

"Afraid not. Small courtesies drummed into me by my dad. Do you mind? It's a new world. I'm never quite sure if someone's going to find it offensive. I did have a lady snap at me once when I opened our office building door for her that she was quite capable of doing it herself."

"Witch," she said.

He grinned. That little dimple popped out in his cheek when he did that. He was wearing a moss green shirt this morning.

The color did wicked things to his eyes.

"That's what I thought, too," Jay said, lightly, "I didn't say it out loud, though."

"But you still open doors, even after that," she said, and something within her sighed with delight at his old-fashioned manners.

"I gauge the recipient," he admitted.

"Well, you gauged this recipient just right," she assured him.

Jolie didn't feel as if she started breathing again until she had settled beside Jay in the passenger seat. How could the very air around her sister and her friends feel so stifling?

She shot him a look.

"What?" he asked her.

"*Are* you cranky this morning?"

"I might have been if you told me you could open your own door," he said, that easy grin deepening his dimple.

This morning's outing—the impossible assignment of finding a dress aside—was as unexpected to her as a prisoner suddenly finding herself escaped from the cell. It seemed as if he was having the same reaction to it.

She sighed with relief. "What a beautiful day. What a beautiful car."

"Thanks, I enjoy it for the few months of the year it's usable in Canada. Top up or down?" he asked her. "We have to choose now. It's not like James Bond. It's not recommended you do it on the fly."

"Down," she said without hesitation.

It was like something out of a dream, whisking along roads that twisted through vineyards and clung to the edge of cliffs that overlooked the sparkling waters of the lake. Jolie was so aware of Jay's complete comfort and confidence behind the wheel. Despite his denial, he could have been James Bond! There was something very sexy about a man who handled a powerful car well, without feeling any need to show off.

After a bit, she took the band out of her hair and let the wind take it. She saw Jay glance over and grin.

"Thatta girl."

"Thank you for suggesting breakfast in town. It minimized the chances of an encounter with Anthony this morning."

"Ha! I can't wait to see the look on The Four's faces when they see two men floundering at your feet."

She hadn't thought of it like that. The wind, as well as being loud, was wreaking havoc on her hair, and with a touch of a button, Jay put the windows up. It helped marginally with the wind, but not at all with the loudness.

"Let's have fun with it," he suggested, and turned on some music. Loud.

"How'd you do that?" she shouted when she recognized music from their high school era.

"Never moved on," he said. "Stuck there. Musically, anyway."

No need to let him know fun did not come naturally to her. She had a sudden sense of being able to be whoever she wanted to be for the next little while.

"And look," he said, "the fun begins right here."

A sign welcomed them to Penticton, the Peach City. They both burst out laughing. She made Jay stop and she deliberately waited for him to come open her door. He did so with flourish and then they stood together under the sign. She took a selfie and sent it to Sabrina.

Should have no problem finding the right shade here.

Penticton, located between two lakes, reminded Jolie a bit of Italy with its dry hills, interspersed with vibrant green terraces of vineyards and orchards. It was a smaller city and the quaint downtown was already thronged with early morning tourists trying to beat the heat of the afternoon.

They found a cute little sidewalk café for breakfast, and sat down. Jolie pulled her hair clip from her pocket, but when she tried to scrape her now really wild hair back to retie it, she noticed Jay was looking at her.

"You should leave it," he said softly.

And so she did.

Jolie looked around and marveled at the unexpected turn her life had taken this morning. She watched the couples, young and old, strolling the streets, the families on vacation. There was a distinctive feeling of summer holiday happiness in the air.

She had heard if you wanted to know who someone really was, to watch how they treated a server in a restaurant.

When the young woman brought coffee, she introduced herself. She apologized for the slow service and confided that one of the waitresses had not come to work.

"Susan, I've been watching you handle things," Jay told her. "You're doing an amazing job."

He said it casually, with just a glance up from the menu, and a quick smile, but to Jolie, as she watched the young woman take on her challenges with new confidence, it told her a great deal about Jay.

A few minutes later they watched Susan rush by with a whipped-cream-and-strawberry-covered waffle that filled the whole plate.

"I wonder if those come in smaller sizes," Jolie said.

"For simplicity's sake, why don't we just share one?"

While they waited for their order to come, Jay read the back of the menu out loud.

"Penticton," he informed her, "was named by the Interior Salish people, and translates to *a place to stay forever.*"

Jolie realized that was exactly what she felt

right now, as if she would like to stay in this simple place—coffee and sunshine, people watching and an appealing companion—forever. She liked the feeling of nothing to prove and nothing to accomplish. She liked her hair being wild around her face, and she liked sitting in the sunshine, being perceived as a couple by others, and feeling like a couple, even though they weren't really.

When their waffle came, it hadn't been divided, and the feeling of being part of a couple deepened as Jolie found herself sitting very close to Jay, eating off the same plate. It seemed to her the moment was infused with an intimacy that was not quite like anything she had ever felt before. Considering she had been engaged for nearly a year, that was very telling of her relationship.

Again, she had that sense of just wanting to stay in this moment, forever, to deepen her connection with him.

"I never met your mom and dad, officially," she told him, "but I often watched them stroll through the neighborhood hand in hand."

"Their evening walk," he said. "It was their ritual. Almost sacred to them. It didn't matter if it was thirty below zero and the wind was blowing, off they went. Every day until he was too sick to do it. You mentioned seeing them walk in the card you sent. I appreciated that."

He remembered something she had written in a card years ago. It didn't necessarily mean anything. He had great people skills. She had just seen that with the young waitress.

"I have another memory of them," she said. "There was a little flower bed in front of your house, between the fence and the sidewalk."

"Mom's flower bed. Her pride and joy," he said, remembering.

"I was on the other side of the street, and I saw her out kneeling in front of it, pulling weeds. And your dad came up behind her and tapped her on the shoulder."

She remembered with absolute clarity, the light that had come on in Millie Fletcher's face when she saw who had tapped her on the shoulder. She had gotten to her feet and wiped her hands on her slacks.

"He had something hidden behind his back," Jolie continued, "and he gave it to her. It was a little bedraggled marigold in a plastic pot, the kind you get for ninety-nine cents at the grocery store. I could hear him say he'd rescued it. Your mother took that pot from him and you would have thought he'd given her a diamond.

"They knelt down side by side and put it in the flower bed right away. It didn't go with a single other thing that was in that bed. But every day, I'd walk by it and see it front and center. I don't know that much about flowers, but the next year, it had thrown seeds or volunteered or whatever it is flowers do, and there were more of them."

She realized at some point Jay had dropped his sunglasses over his eyes. He was looking away from her, and didn't say anything when she finished the story. She realized, horrified, that she had hurt him.

"I'm sorry," she said. "I've said something wrong."

"No, not at all," he said. "That's just exactly what they were like."

He lifted the glasses and squeezed the bridge of his nose.

She remembered, then seeing it so clearly last night, after he'd rescued her from Anthony. That it had all fallen on him.

"Jay?" she asked softly. "Why don't you tell me about it?"

He hesitated, taking a sip of his coffee. Then he lifted a shoulder.

"My mom never recovered," he said in a low voice, studying his plate. "She's lost without him. I was nearly grown-up, but I had younger siblings still at home. It didn't matter. Nothing mattered. She's like a shell. That flower bed you mentioned? She hasn't touched it for years now. It's a mess. Like the whole family."

"You held it all together, didn't you?"

He was still looking at their plate. "As much as I was able."

"You're a good man, Jay Fletcher." That came from the bottom of her heart.

He lifted his eyes and looked at her for a moment. She felt the deepest of connections shiver along her spine.

But then he dropped his sunglasses, and smiled.

"I don't want to be a pig," Jay said, eager to change the subject, "but I'd like another one. How about you?"

"I wouldn't normally say yes, but *pig* rhymes with *fig*, so I think it would be fine."

They both laughed, and it seemed they had moved on from the intensity of the moment when he had confided in her about his family, but she was aware of the connection remaining in some subtle, lovely way.

Sharing a second waffle with him proved as impossible to say no to as the prosecco had been last night.

They had just finished the second waffle, when her phone notified her with Sabrina's distinctive ping.

The feeling of intimacy she had been enjoying dissolved as reality intruded.

"Duty calls," she said, wagging her phone at Jay.

He grimaced.

"Ah, yes, dress instructions," she said.

"I was hoping to hold out for the fig leaf."

"Only if they come in peach," she told him sternly.

"Pigs are not peaches," he informed her, just as sternly. "Sorry, I meant figs."

She giggled. She had never really been *that* girl. The one who giggled. She was surprised by how much she liked it.

She glanced at the photos Sabrina had sent of Beth and Jack and Jill in their dresses. Like the bridesmaids themselves—except for her—the dresses were variations on a theme. The continuity factor was the peach color.

She showed the photo to Jay.

He wrinkled his nose. "Horrible color."

"Probably devilishly difficult to find."

"We could buy some construction paper," he said with a snap of his fingers, "and make it. Peach-colored fig leaves. One for me. Three for you."

She smacked him on the arm, and he pretended he was gravely wounded. She noticed an older woman smiling at them indulgently.

Assuming they were a couple.

Maybe that assumption was part of what made it so easy to reach for his hand as they navigated the busy streets on their quest for peach dresses. Or maybe it was the lingering effect of him trusting her with his broken heart.

They tried shop after shop. She couldn't help but notice how Jay treated people, with a kind of friendly respect that they responded to. Of course, a few of those women in those shops were just responding to his green eyes and dimpled grin!

Still, the search for the dress proved both exhausting and fruitless. There was apparently, not a peach dress to be found in the entire Peach City.

"I'm going to single-handedly ruin my sister's wedding photos," she told Jay.

"I think we should sue Penticton for false advertising."

"But the stay forever part is true," she said, and heard the wistfulness in her own voice.

He looked at her long and hard. "Yes," he finally said, "that part is true."

"Why don't you try a bridal shop?" the clerk in one of the stores suggested. "We have three."

She marked all three of them on a map for Jay and Jolie.

"If this doesn't work out," Jolie said, "I could try online. Sometimes delivery is shockingly fast."

"It's always good to have a backup plan," Jay agreed, as they found the first of the bridal stores.

He stepped in the door first. "Every man's worst nightmare. I think a fairy tale exploded in here. I'm drowning in unrealistic romantic dreams."

She saw the remark in a completely different way since he had shared his family tragedy with her. He was running away from the thing that had brought his family pain—love. And who could blame him?

"It's pretty estrogen rich," Jolie agreed, keeping it light.

She explained her mission to the clerk, who shook her head. No peach dresses. The second and third shops were also strikeouts.

But before they left, Jay squinted at a rack. "I'm no expert on colors, but I could swear that dress over there is the same shade you had on last night."

"Oh, that's not a dress," the clerk said, "It's an underslip."

"It looks like a dress to me," Jay said, moving over to the rack. He pulled out the slip on its hangar and held it out for Jolie's inspection.

"It's not a dress," she told him firmly. "It goes under a dress. Like a petticoat."

"I know what a slip is," he said wryly.

Of course he did! A man like this was likely quite familiar with what women wore under their clothes.

"It looks pretty sheer," Jolie said, doubtfully.

"Oh," he said pleased, "the next best thing to a fig leaf."

In some way, the item he was holding up reminded her of her wedding gown, probably because of its cut and pure simplicity. It was also silk.

"Put it back," she said. She thought she probably shouldn't try that on, but she heard the lack of conviction in her voice. For some reason it was like having more prosecco and another waffle. Irresistible.

"I think you should at least try it. You know, in the interest of having fun. And a backup plan."

Plus, it made her feel as if she would appear to be stiff and uptight if she refused. Oh, who was she kidding? She *was* stiff and up tight. But not today.

Today, she was a carefree woman who had wind-tangled hair and a handsome man at her side, and the whole world felt completely different than it had twenty-four hours ago.

CHAPTER EIGHT

"FINE," JOLIE CAPITULATED. "I'll try it on and you can see for yourself how inappropriate it would be."

"Oh," Jay said, wagging a wicked eyebrow at her, "I do love me some inappropriate."

She snatched the fabric out of his hands, and marched to the change room. What would it hurt?

She took off her clothes, and slid the silky chemise over her head. Just like last night, her underwear did nothing for it. The fabric was unforgiving of every line. She hesitated then took off her underwear and put the sheath back on.

It floated over her naked skin as sensual as a touch.

She turned and looked at herself in the mirror. She was stunned by the woman who looked back at her: bold and playful and daring. The slip hugged her in places, but it skimmed in others, hinting at what lay beneath.

She had to admit Jay had an eye. The slip was

astonishing. Unlike the monstrosity of a dress last night, she looked absolutely gorgeous in it.

Taking a deep breath, encouraging the newer bolder "fun" girl to come out to play, she opened the change room door and stepped out.

Jay went stock-still. The only thing that moved was his Adam's apple, which bobbed in his throat when he swallowed.

"See?" she said, doing a twirl. "It's way too—"

"You," he croaked.

The saleslady came and looked at her. Her eyes widened with appreciation.

"You know, not everyone could pull that off, but you can. Slip dresses look like this one, cut on the bias, with spaghetti straps. They are actually very vogue right now."

"It's almost see-through," Jolie protested.

Jay grinned wickedly. "Fig leafs here we come."

"If I quickly stitched another slip inside of it, it would be absolutely perfect," the sales associate suggested, "but it will still cling a bit, so it depends how comfortable you are going without underwear."

"Commando," Jay filled in helpfully.

"Commando?" Jolie asked.

"That's what it's called. Going without underwear."

"You're a surprising expert on the topic," Jolie teased him, aware of how nice it felt to tease a man.

"Stick with me. I'm full of surprises."

For a woman who had avoided surprises, at all costs, for almost her entire life, she was not sure why that sounded quite so enticing.

"Just take it off," the saleslady suggested, "put on that housecoat behind the door and let me see what I can do with it."

Jolie looked back in the mirror. The chemise was just way too sexy. It was way too bold. Still, it was one hundred and fifty percent better than the other dress.

"Okay," she agreed, part reluctance and part hope. She retreated back to the change room, came out in an oversize fluffy white housecoat and handed the scrap of fabric to the clerk, who whisked it away to another room.

Now she was standing in a bridal shop, in a housecoat with not a stitch on underneath it. She was not sure why that felt even more intimate than standing before Jay in the crazy dress that wasn't really a dress but underwear, but it did.

Jay stared at Jolie. He felt absolutely terrified. It felt as if his mission—to show her who she really was—was going completely off the rails and leading him into dark overgrown forests where it was possible dragons lurked.

It had started when he had encouraged her to leave her hair down.

And then sharing that waffle with her had been strangely erotic.

But the worst thing of all had been telling her about his destroyed family. He'd never unburdened to anyone before.

He was aware that it should have felt like a weakness revealing that kind of information to someone who realistically was a stranger to him.

Except she didn't feel like a stranger.

He *knew* her. He'd known her since she was a kid.

Maybe it had just felt safe to confide in Jolie because their reacquaintance promised to be a short one. She would go back to Italy. He would go back to the blessed distractions of working too much.

The underwear dress she had been wearing was the epitome of what the mission was all about. To show her how bold and sexy she was. To make her not afraid of that.

But maybe he was the one who was going to have to be afraid.

Because all these things felt as if he was uncovering, subtly and slowly, layers that hid the real her.

But this—Jolie standing in front of him in a housecoat—felt as if everything had been stripped away, and what remained was purely her.

How could the housecoat—the white thick terry cloth kind that you got in upscale hotels—be even more revealing than the underslip had been?

This was the stunning truth: she was beautiful, she was brilliant and she was kind. He could feel himself leaning toward the softness he had seen in her eyes when he had revealed the truth about his family like a sailor looking for refuge from a storm-tossed sea.

The thing about *her*—with her wild hair and her cheeky smile, and the way she could rock lingerie as if it was a dress, but especially her, standing before him in a simple white housecoat—was that he could picture her in his future.

In his kitchen.

The morning after.

In his life for a lot of morning afters.

Maybe it was because of the backdrop of row after row of pure white wedding dresses that he could hear the word *forever* in his mind as if it had been spoken out loud.

Everything was getting all mixed up inside his head. He was trying to show her who she really was.

But he had known from the beginning that there was a danger of him not being able to handle that.

Of him finding out who he really was instead.

And it was, terrifyingly, someone who still wanted to believe in what he saw shining in her eyes.

Despite the fact Jay had plenty of evidence to the contrary, something about Jolie seemed to overshadow that evidence.

That tomorrow would be okay, after all.

He was aware that he had to put the brakes on, right now, before he drove them both over a cliff.

The clerk returned with the peach-colored scrap of fabric. She had transformed it into a dress with another slip stitched expertly to the inside of the original.

When Jolie came out the second time, it felt as if the wind was knocked from him, like when he played hockey and suddenly found himself on the ice, staring at the ceiling, unable to breathe, wondering what the heck had happened.

He deliberately kept his features bland, even though he had to fight the guy who wanted to flounder at her feet.

"That's the one," he said, and then glanced at his watch. "Where has the day gone? Wow, it's nearly four thirty. We've got to go. Troy was supposed to arrive this afternoon and I have some business phone calls I have to make."

It would be very late in the Eastern part of Canada to be making calls, but people were used to hearing from him at all hours.

Business, his refuge.

His sister called him a workaholic. As if that was a bad thing!

He was a workaholic for a reason! Because work was predictable, and allowed him to be in control.

Unlike family. That sister, who was so fond of calling him commitment phobic and a workaholic, had been fifteen when their father had died. She had desperately needed a mom to guide her through that time.

Instead, it had been on him. And he'd been clumsy and ill-prepared to be the one who said, *No, you're too young to date*, and *No, you can't wear your makeup like that*, and *No*—actually that one had been *Absolutely no—you can't wear that outfit*.

Begging his mom to weigh in, begging her to come back to them.

But no, it had been Troy who had been his wingman through it all. Being there when Mike had come home drunk, and Jim had gotten in the accident with the motorbike he'd acquired on the sly.

Troy had a way of *seeing* people. It was as if he could see right through their faults and foibles to their souls, Sabrina being a prime example of that.

Watching how Troy dealt with people had helped Jay come to terms with the confusion of feelings around his mom, softened him toward her.

But what had not softened was his fierce decision that he would never put his own heart in a position to be so broken by love.

A resolve he had to firm up right now!

He put the roof of the convertible up for the trip back to Hidden Valley. He was not sure, after having seen Jolie in that dress, that he could stand watching the wind blow in her hair again. It made a man want to comb through those tangles with his hands.

Which made him think of that kiss they had shared last night.

No, things were getting way, way too complicated between him and little Miss Cavaletti.

He steeled himself against her look of disappointment.

"It's too hot," he said. "Bad for the upholstery. Not to mention heatstroke. You would not believe how many people get heatstroke in convertibles, from that sun beating down on their heads."

He should have thought it through more carefully, though, about putting the top up, because now they could hear each other. He didn't want to make any more conversation with her. It felt as if she could pull his secrets from him like a magnet held above steel filings.

He didn't put the nostalgic tunes back on. He chose classical.

And blasted it.

And pretended to be oblivious to the fact his sudden withdrawal was hurting her.

Better to hurt her now than later.

Because his mother and father had shown him what the future held if you loved someone too deeply.

There it was.

Jolie Cavaletti invited a man to love deeply, to want things he had already decided it was best that he didn't have.

And he had to protect both of them from those kinds of desires.

Desire. Another complication rearing its ugly head, the element that could guarantee a man could not think straight about anything. Her hair, her lips, the way she had looked in that lingerie? He probably wasn't going to have a sensible thought until after the wedding.

Never mind his mission to show her who she was.

In that little piece of fabric that had somehow been transformed into a dress?

It would be perfectly evident to anyone who wasn't blind exactly who Jolie was.

From the moment Jolie emerged from the changing room, she sensed something was different, that she was back to being on her own. Jay was gone. She took the dress to the front counter.

"You did such a good job, thank you."

"You're welcome." The clerk waved away her credit card. "It's paid for."

Jay was outside, scrolling through his phone.

"You shouldn't have paid for the dress," she told him.

"I wanted to."

"Well, you shouldn't have. It's not the same as holding open a door for someone. You already paid for breakfast. What do I owe you?"

"Your firstborn?"

"I'm not kidding, Jay."

He looked annoyed, but he gave her the amount, and she settled up with him.

After that, Jolie could feel the chill, and it wasn't coming just from the fact that Jay, apparently worried about heatstroke, had the air conditioner in the car going full blast.

No, he was pulling away from her. It was in the set of his shoulders and jaw, in the line of his lips, in the way he was focused so intently—too intently—on the road, as if he was driving in a Formula 1 event. She tried to think what she might have done to bring on this distressing shift in attitude, but she came up blank. Surely it wasn't about her paying her own way?

Still, there was no mistaking the fact he had

gone from warm and charming to remote in the blink of an eye.

It hurt.

But it shouldn't. No! She should be grateful to him. When they had come out of the store and it had been so hot she felt like butter about to melt, she had entertained the notion that they would stop at one of the many beaches they had passed on the way to Penticton and have a swim.

She didn't have a bathing suit with her and he didn't, either, as far as she knew, so what had she been thinking might happen?

A skinny-dip at a secluded beach somewhere?

That was what happened when you just let your hair blow around willy-nilly and were persuaded to try on slips and pass them off as dresses.

That was what happened when you stood before a man with only the thinnest of silky barriers separating your nakedness from him.

Boldness could become a drug, constantly pushing you to go further and further!

She was just getting over one relationship. She certainly did not need to be falling for another guy. Standing before him in skimpy clothing, relishing the look in his eyes, entertaining ideas of skinny-dipping on a hot day.

She slid Jay a look.

Was she falling for him?

How was that even possible? Her logical mind

did not like it. Their reunion was not even twenty-four hours old.

That was chemistry, for you. Or maybe it was biology. Or some powerful combination of the two. But, realistically, how much of the present was being influenced by her feelings for Jay from the past?

So, no, she was not. Falling. Falling suggested a certain lack of control, something that *happened* to you, instead of something you chose.

She was too close to her last romantic fiasco to be making the same errors all over again. If she did ever choose another relationship—a big *if*—she decided she would take a scientific approach to it. Emotions could not be trusted.

Jay had done her a favor by keeping the roof up and blasting her with cold air and his own chilliness all the way home. A huge favor.

They arrived back at Hidden Valley, and she got out of the car, not giving him a chance to open the door for her. Who needed that? New independent Jolie did not need old-fashioned shows of chivalry!

She managed, just barely, to refrain from saying, *I can open the door myself.*

"Thanks for a nice day," she said instead, a woman grateful for the huge favor that had been bestowed on her. Why did she sound faintly snippy?

She gathered up her parcel and her purse. She

tossed her tangle of hair over her shoulder and *liked* the look on his face, his chilliness momentarily pierced by an ice-melting look of heat.

Or maybe that was actual heat she was feeling. Leaving the car felt as though she was entering a blast furnace. It had probably been very wise of him to leave the top of the car up.

She didn't spare him another glance. She closed the door—technically, it might have been a slam— and then she moved away from his car and quickly toward the relative sanctuary of her cabin.

With its stupid name that conjured up all kinds of unlikely possibilities.

CHAPTER NINE

ANTHONY HAD THE exceedingly poor judgment to intercept Jolie as she aimed for the shade that surrounded her cabin. "I've been looking for you all day."

Jolie glanced around for her accidental fiancé and saw that he and Troy had met up and, towels over their shoulders, were walking down toward the lake.

Getting the swim she had wanted.

She didn't need a man to rescue her!

"Get out of my way," she snapped in Italian when Anthony looked as if he intended to block her path.

She was aware her annoyance might have had a little more to do with being iced out by Jay than Anthony showing up.

And the heat.

Italians had the good sense to have *riposa* in the midday heat.

Undeterred—maybe not reading her mood, he

had never been particularly sensitive to others—Anthony matched his stride to hers.

"You've had a fight," he said with satisfaction.

So, he read more into her than she had given him credit for. Still, how dare he think she was going to confide the personal details of her life to him?

"Go away," she said, still in Italian. "Go home. You're not welcome here."

"That's not what your sister said," he replied smoothly.

She did an about-face. Despite the temptations of the shade and her little cottage nestled in those towering trees, Jolie didn't actually want Anthony trailing her all the way to her cabin. It would be better if he didn't even know which one she was in.

Lovers' Retreat. He might see that as some kind of invitation. Who named these places, anyway?

She walked back to the lodge. and stopped at the desk. "Which room is my sister in? Sabrina Cavaletti?"

At least she knew her sister wasn't having a reunion with her husband-to-be, because she had just seen him.

She knew many large hotels would never give out a room number, but there were no such problems at the cozy, smaller lodge, and they gave her Sabrina's room information. Anthony trailed in the door behind her.

"If he asks," she said in a stern undertone, "do not, under any circumstances, tell him which cabin I am in."

She could tell by the guilty look on the clerk's face that it was too late.

She turned and glared at Anthony. "Vamoose," she snapped.

He stopped, gave her a hangdog look, as if somehow he was the victim, then turned and walked away.

Jolie hammered on Sabrina's door. Her sister apparently approved of *riposa* because she was not only in, but in her housecoat.

She had some kind of terrible mud mask on her face. The mud mask looked like something from a horror film, green and dripping, at the same time as being one of those *girl* things that Jolie was excluded from. She glanced over her sister's shoulder. She was alone.

"How could you?" Jolie demanded, without preamble. "You knew I'd broken up with Anthony. Why would you invite him here?"

Sabrina gestured her in, and closed the door behind her. She regarded her for a moment.

"Your hair looks as if you've survived a tornado."

This from a woman with green slime melting off her face! So tempting to say *Jay likes it*. Tempting, childish and off topic.

"How could you?" Jolie repeated.

"He tracked me down online. He told me it was just a spat and that you were being stubborn, which I mean, literally, you *can* be stubborn, Jolie! Mom and I both liked him so much when we met him last year in Italy, and he was being so charming. I thought it was quite romantic how determined he was to be with you. Mom and I think he's perfect for you."

"You and Mom don't have any say in my life."

"Thank you. That's more than obvious since you've chosen to live about a million miles away from us."

Jolie registered that her sister sounded hurt. "Seven thousand kilometers."

Sabrina rolled her eyes. "Anyway, he's a nice guy and very good-looking and he has a job."

"Is that where you set the bar?"

"After I spoke with him, I was convinced it would be right for you to give him another chance."

"No."

"Why not? You were crazy about him. Where did that go?"

"The most correct word in there is *crazy*. I was crazy."

"But what happened?"

"He cheated on me! And that's a pattern from

our childhood that I will not repeat. For goodness' sake, Mom named me after a song where a woman is *begging* another woman to quit having an affair with her man."

"That song was called 'Jolene,' and you're Jolie."

"I think we both know what she meant. By changing a few letters she was trying to, like, have a secret code. It's pathetic. I won't ever be like that."

Her sister looked genuinely stunned. "Jolie, I'm sorry, I had no idea."

"About the song, or Anthony?"

"I hate that song. Every time it's resurrected by another singer, I want to say, *For heaven's sake, take him already.* I just never would have pictured Anthony being that kind of guy."

"Me, either," Jolie said glumly.

"Are you sure?" Sabrina asked.

"Of course, I'm sure. I saw him in the gelato shop making kissy faces over a dish of *spaghettieis.*"

"Is that the ice cream dish that looks like spaghetti and meatballs?"

Jolie nodded.

"But that's your favorite," Sabrina breathed.

"Anthony introduced me to it."

"You didn't have a clue?" Sabrina asked with a tiny bit of insulting skepticism. "You didn't see him making eyes at the servers when you went out for dinner?"

"We hadn't been out much. When I saw him with that other woman, he actually blamed me. He said I focused too much on work."

"Why, that snake!" And then, "Jolie, why didn't you tell me?"

"I just wanted to nurse my bruised dignity in private without you and Mom kicking around my misery like a football with not enough air in it."

"It's very hurtful that you have such a low opinion of Mom and me."

"How is this suddenly about you?"

Her sister sighed. "The same ice cream dish he wooed you with. That is beyond low."

"Yes, *snake* kind of implies that."

"What did you do?"

"I walked away, of course, and sent him a text. That I had seen him and that it was over. Then I blocked him."

"He would have been wearing that ice cream, if it was me. I'll tell him to leave."

"Thank you. I just told him to leave, but I don't think he's going to listen to me."

"I'm really sorry, Jolie. I wish you would have told me sooner."

There was no nice way to say you did not trust your sister with your innermost secrets.

Sabrina unfortunately proved that assessment

was probably correct when she seized on the package Jolie was still carrying, and seemed ready to leave the topic of her sister's heartbreak and humiliation behind with barely a pause.

But then Sabrina surprised Jolie by pulling out her phone and scrolling through it. "Here's the messages from him." She tapped in furiously. "There! I've told him to leave. Right now."

"Thank you."

"What's going on between you and Jay?" Sabrina asked, surprising Jolie further by actually showing some interest in her life "That kiss this morning gave us all a bit of a shock."

Interest, then, or judgment? Did they not see her in Jay's league? Well, let them wonder!

"Did it?" she said smoothly.

Sabrina chewed on her lip, struggling between wanting details, and trying to make up for the fact she'd invited her sister's philandering fiancé to her wedding.

"You got a dress!" Sabrina said, wisely putting both Jay's kiss and the debacle with Anthony behind her.

"Yes, I did." She slid it from the package.

"The color! Perfect. The fabric, though. Never mind. Try it on for me," Sabrina insisted, and shoved Jolie toward the washroom.

Jolie put on the remade chemise again. Somehow, she didn't feel it was nearly as much fun as it had been modeling it for Jay.

She stepped out of the hotel room bathroom self-consciously.

Her sister stared at her. Her mouth fell open, and then she closed it. "You can't wear that," she said firmly.

"It's that obvious?" Jolie asked.

"Obvious?"

"That it's an underslip?"

Sabrina frowned, came over and took a closer look. "I would have never guessed that, actually. It looks like the cutest ever little sundress."

"But then—"

"Hey, on Saturday there is one star of the show, and that's me. If you wear that dress, all eyes will be on you. You look stunning. You should dress like that more often. Just not at my wedding."

And then her sister actually smiled at her.

"If I wear the other dress all eyes will be on me, too," Jolie pointed out.

"Sadly, true. Such a disaster. I was trying to find all different dresses with the same color. I ordered them online. I didn't even notice the worms."

"Snakes," Jolie corrected her, and Sabrina snorted back a laugh.

"I think we've discussed snakes quite enough for one day," Sabrina said.

"Maybe you can find something else online. Delivery can be mind-blowingly quick. Thanks for saying I look stunning. You've never said that to me before."

"You know what? One sister is supposed to be the smart one, and one is supposed to be the pretty one, and I'm annoyed—super annoyed, actually—that you're both."

"I always thought you were the pretty one," Jolie said. Sabrina cast herself down on the bed and Jolie joined her.

"That would depend who you asked. You were always Dad's favorite."

"And you were Mom's," she said, feeling the sadness of two sisters in divided camps.

"I was the reason him and Mom had to get married. That came up in every fight. That she *trapped* him."

"I'm sorry."

"It's got nothing to do with you," her sister said, a little too sharply. "Anyway, who knows if that's why you were his favorite. You looked like him. And then, when you were eight or something, you started speaking Italian, just out of the blue, as if it was no big deal."

If Sabrina was a tiny bit mean to her sometimes, wasn't there an explanation for it?

"I'm afraid *vamoose* is about the limit of my Italian," Sabrina confessed.

"It's Spanish, actually, from a Latin root."

"See? That's exactly what I mean! Who knows the Latin root of *vamoose*?"

"From *vadimus*."

"Or that Italy is seven thousand miles away."

"Kilometers."

"You're such a geek, Jolie. That's why I was literally so happy for you when you found Anthony. He seemed kind of normal. But maybe you should just stick to the geeks."

Which Jay most definitely did not qualify as.

"You don't have to say that as if I'm nothing without a man. It's a little too much like that song. I've decided I won't be doing the romance thing again."

"Huh. Well, that might be one area where I'm smarter than you, sis. Because you don't choose love, it chooses you. If I could choose, do you think I'd choose Troy again? But I love him."

"What happened between you? Please don't tell me he cheated."

"Troy? Never. But we just fought all the time. Then I said I wanted a baby, he said he wasn't ready. No, he said *we* weren't ready. He finally said he'd had enough, and he wasn't bringing any poor, unsuspecting kid into a war zone. It kind of blindsided me because I didn't think it was *that* bad."

"Did you consider the fact that you were comfortable with fighting because that's what you grew up with? Maybe you actually believe that's how things get solved."

"I didn't know your degree was in psychiatry, Doc."

"Our childhoods shape us, whether we like it or not. I wonder how much our childhood had to do with me picking a philanderer."

"Seriously, Jolie, a philanderer?"

Jolie realized, resigned, her sister was commenting on her vocabulary not her choice of men. If you can't beat them, join them, she thought.

Sabrina's phone quacked.

"Mom?" Jolie asked.

"How did you know?"

"I assigned her the same tone."

They laughed together. It actually felt like they might have a sisterly bond.

Sabrina looked at her phone. "She's not arriving now until the day before the wedding."

Jolie thought her sister looked relieved.

"She says Dad's coming with her."

"Together?"

"It sounds like it."

"Reconciliation," both women said together, and not happily.

"You see, if you could choose, who would choose that?" Sabrina asked.

Who indeed? Jolie thought. Her childhood

peppered with her dad leaving and her mother begging him to come back.

And she still was? All these years later? Jolie hadn't known it was still going on. She felt faintly guilty about leaving her sister alone with the family drama.

"Do you have an extra one of those? The thing on your face?"

"I do. But go take off the dress first. I don't want it to get wrecked. Just in case."

They actually had a somewhat sisterly moment while Sabrina applied the mask to her face.

"Avocado. It's miraculous."

Jolie refrained from asking to see the pouch it came in so she could study the ingredients. Instead, she allowed herself to enjoy Sabrina's pampering.

"It needs to stay on for one hour," her sister instructed her, in her wheelhouse now, doing exactly the kind of girly things that Jolie had never been able to figure out the appeal of. "If you wash it off right before supper, you'll see. Magic."

Jolie was more interested in the science behind the product than the magic, but it would probably spoil the moment if she said so. Plus, her sister did have enviably fabulous skin, like porcelain.

"Ta-da." Sabrina held up a mirror and Jolie's mouth dropped open.

"I think there was a perfectly terrible movie starring this character."

"It'll be worth it, you'll see."

"You mean I have to walk through the resort looking like this?"

"Maybe Anthony will see you and be dissuaded."

It wasn't actually Anthony seeing her that she was worried about!

CHAPTER TEN

JOLIE SHARED A laugh with her sister, as if it really was Anthony she was afraid of seeing, and not Jay. She tried, without success, to remember when the last time she had laughed with her sister was.

"Remember, one hour," Sabrina called after her.

Jolie managed to get back to her cabin without anyone noticing her. She was fairly certain she left a trail of melting green globs behind her.

The heat was insufferable.

The cabin, thankfully, was in the trees, cool and dark inside.

She looked at herself in the mirror, horrified. Was she really supposed to wear this for an hour? Her skin already felt weirdly tight. She tapped the goop. Was it hardening at the edges? Would her sister ever know if she washed it off right now?

But somehow that felt like a betrayal of Sabrina's efforts, not to mention that somehow the idea of softly glowing skin, in the face of being spurned by Jay, was too appealing to resist.

Spurned was probably too strong a word. She

had been imagining a naked swim for two, he had been preoccupied with business. She probably wouldn't have had the nerve, even if the opportunity had presented itself.

Anthony was all the evidence she needed that she was not good at reading the subtle signals men were sending out.

Jolie suddenly felt exhausted. She glanced at her watch. No wonder she was tired. It was the middle of the night in Italy.

She knew the wrong thing to do was to give in to jet lag. You were supposed to tough it out.

She wouldn't have a sleep, she told herself just a little *riposa*, that was all. She'd just close her eyes for a few minutes. She set the alarm on her phone.

She went and took off her skirt, slipped her bra out from under her blouse, and laid down in her bed, on her back, so she wouldn't spoil the sheets with the green goop. Her bedroom window was open and a hot breeze blew over her.

She fell asleep almost instantly.

Jolie woke up feeling disoriented. The scent of avocado was heavy in the air, it was pitch black and she had no idea where she was. It felt as if something was encasing her face. With faint panic, she reached up and encountered a hard surface.

Slowly it came back to her.

Canada.

Her sister's wedding.

Green goop hardened on her face in the interest of glowing beauty.

Jay.

The reason for her sudden interest in glowing beauty.

"He can like me the way I am or not at all," she said, glancing at her watch. Of course, if the ride home from Penticton was any indication, he had chosen not at all.

Still, a woman wanted to be at her best when she'd been rejected.

It was past midnight. What had happened to her alarm? She had missed dinner. It had been a terrible mistake to give in to that desire to rest. She would be completely turned around now. She made herself stay in bed. She clenched her eyes firmly shut, and ordered herself to slumber.

Instead, she remembered the day. In detail.

She heard a sound outside her cabin and the hair rose on the back of her neck. First, branches broke, and then there was a groaning sound.

There was a wild animal out there. She was certain it was a bear. Toronto did not have bears, but this part of the world did.

Wasn't there even a warning on the garbage cans?

She'd heard bears had very sensitive noses.

She didn't have any food in the cabin, but maybe it was being drawn to the scent of avocado. If she could smell avocado—and she could—surely a bear could, too.

"Don't be so dramatic," she ordered herself. It didn't have to be bear. It could be something smaller. Like a raccoon.

Or a mountain lion.

Heart pounding, being so quiet that the night creature, whatever it was, wouldn't be able to determine there was an edible person along with the avocado in her cabin, she slid over to the window and peered out.

Her eyes slowly adjusted to the dark. The moon was out and reflected off the lake. Under different circumstances she might see it as beautiful.

Another branch snapped. And another groan came.

Was she relieved it was Anthony? She was pretty sure she would have preferred any one of the other possibilities. He was placing himself, with a singular lack of grace, on a perch amongst the tangled branches of a large lilac shrub.

She squinted at him. What was that in his hand?

Oh, please, no. It was a guitar. The instrument looked like it may have been a toy. He strummed it thoughtfully. The sound seemed amplified by the pure quiet of the night.

It was worse than a nightmare. Anthony cleared his throat, strummed again and began to sing.

He sang, badly, in Italian. When she first heard her name, she thought it was going to be the song her mother had named her after.

But no, there were, unbelievably, more awful things than that. The song was obviously of his own creation.

It was a ballad about a misunderstood man, and one little mistake. The chorus involved *spaghettieis*, heartbreak—his—and the future children that he hoped would possess Jolie's eyes.

Such was the nature of jet lag that she pictured unruly children carrying between them a bag of eyes.

The caterwauling continued, unabated. Thankfully, her cabin was fairly isolated. There was one next door, but yesterday it had not looked occupied.

Her relief at not disturbing the neighbors—not having witnesses to the serenade—was short-lived. The cabin next door was apparently occupied now, because she saw a light come on.

She took a deep breath, ducked into her bedroom and looked around for the skirt she had abandoned earlier. She was not going out there dressed in only a blouse to shock the new neighbors even further.

Just as she bent to pick it up off the floor, she

heard the back door of her cabin open. She froze, realizing she hadn't locked it. Hidden Valley did not seem like the type of place where things had to be locked.

Anthony was inside!

But no, he wasn't, because the singing continued at the front of the cabin.

She peered around the door of her bedroom and discovered it was Jay who stood there.

He glanced her way. Too dark thankfully for him to see her face, or hopefully to notice she was only in her blouse. Who was she kidding that she would have gone skinny-dipping at the first opportunity?

She was going to duck back behind the door, but what he did next paralyzed her so completely she thought maybe even her breathing had stopped.

Jay's fingers moved to the buttons of his shirt. Her mouth went dry as he dispensed them quickly and peeled off that garment.

She had seen the statue of *David* with her own eyes, and it had nothing on Jay Fletcher. Painted in moonlight, it was obvious he was as beautifully and perfectly made as that marble statue. He was one hundred percent pure man—broad shouldered, deep chested, his stomach a hard hollow.

She couldn't have moved now if she wanted to. She got what he was doing. Jolie thought Jay's half nudity would be ample to persuade Anthony they were in the cabin together. Lovers.

At *Lovers' Retreat.*

This had to be a dream, but no, when she pinched herself Jay was still there, and it was apparent he didn't do anything by halves.

With a quick bend and a flick of his wrist, he divested himself of his shorts and Jay Fletcher was standing in her cabin, completely unself-conscious, in just his boxer briefs.

He was magnificent, so much so that the serenade outside her cabin faded in her mind.

While her gaze was glued to him, he barely spared her a glance as he strode through her small living area. Just before he threw open the French door to the balcony, he paused and tousled his hair.

Nice touch. Making it look as if he was here. With her. Unclothed. And messy-haired.

A picture *did* paint a thousand words.

Thank goodness he stepped out, because her face turned so hot she could feel the mask softening.

"Hey," he called from the balcony. "What are you doing, man?"

Anthony' voice and the guitar strumming stopped abruptly. Jolie crept to her bedroom window and watched.

"I will win her back," he cried in English. And then added in Italian, "I am the better man."

"You aren't," she called from the window in Italian. "*He* performs like a stallion."

"You're embarrassing yourself," Jay said to Anthony, almost gently.

Anthony looked to the balcony, and then to the window, and then back again. His shoulders slumped in defeat, and he dropped the guitar. It landed with a sad twang as he shuffled away.

Jolie found her skirt, pulled it on, and slipped into the bathroom. Her face looked horrible! She took a washcloth, soaked it, scrubbed.

Everything looked worse! It wasn't coming off!

"Okay in there?" he called.

"Uh, yeah." She rubbed some more. Her face was a mess, green mask slimy-looking now, but still clinging. "Thank you for the rescue. There's no need to hang around. I don't know how you happened to know I was in need, but thanks."

"I'm in the cottage next door. I heard him. I couldn't resist rescuing a damsel in distress."

Suddenly, he was standing in the hallway, looking through the ajar bathroom door at her.

His mouth fell open.

She tried to laugh it off. "You think you're getting a damsel in distress, and you get the Grinch who stole Christmas instead."

It felt as if she had planted her whole face in a

newly poured sidewalk. Jay came into the bathroom and regarded her thoughtfully. He was trying not to laugh and, thankfully, he succeeded.

He took her chin in his hands and turned her face.

"What the hell have you done to yourself?"

Oh, geez, sharing her cottage with arguably the world's most attractive man, and she looked like this?

"I'm rehearsing for my part as Fiona," she told him.

He looked blank.

"*Shrek*?" One of her favorite movies, where in the end, Fiona is loved for who she is most comfortable being.

He still looked blank. She realized she'd love to curl up with him, a bowl of popcorn, and that movie.

"Sabrina and I had a little girl time when I got back from Penticton. It's an avocado mask. It's supposed to work magic on my skin."

"Your skin did not need any magic worked on it," he told her gruffly.

She sighed inwardly, and Jay reached out tentatively and touched the edge of the mask around her mouth.

His fingers brushed that vulnerable surface.

Don't swoon, she ordered herself. *Friends!*

This could only happen to her. Instead of im-

pressing Jay with her glowing skin, she was looking like the monster from the green lagoon. And
this followed being subjected to the worst serenade by a spurned lover in the history of man-
kind. It was too awkward for words.

Really? Why wasn't he cutting and running?

Because he had decided they could safely be
friends?

CHAPTER ELEVEN

A GREEN CHUNK of her face mask peeled off beneath Jay's fingertips. He studied it as if it was a specimen in those long-ago science classes they had shared.

"Is it edible?" he asked solemnly.

"I didn't have a chance to study the ingredients, but I doubt it."

He put the piece in his mouth and crunched down on it. "Edible," he declared. "Let's face it."

She laughed at his pun and she realized that's what he'd intended. He sensed her awkwardness and was trying to put her at ease.

It was so nice. *Friendly.*

"I might not go as far as edible, it could have hydrogen peroxide in it, and chemicals from fragrances and dyes."

"Will you save me if I topple over?" he asked, seriously.

"I will," she promised, "but at the moment I may be the one needing saving. I've left it on far too long, and it's hurting my face. It was supposed to be an hour. I think it's been closer to seven."

He touched her face with his finger, and then tried to get his fingernail under the mask. He pried gently.

"Ouch."

"I don't think that's supposed to be stuck on like that. I think we better try and get it off."

"I've been trying to get if off."

"I hope we don't need a chisel."

We? Oh, geez, wasn't this just the story of her life? She imagined skinny-dipping and instead got green goo turned to cement being chiseled off her face.

"I'll deal with it. You go."

She turned away from him and scraped at her face with the wet cloth. She yelped a little when the mask resisted, stubbornly glued to her skin.

Jay had not taken his cue, merely leaning one deliciously naked shoulder against the door-frame. After watching her for a few seconds, he came up behind her and took the washcloth from her hand.

If she had thought eating waffles with him and being with him in nothing more than a house-coat had been oddly intimate, those moments were nothing compared to this, him at such close quarters in such a tiny space.

He dabbed at her face. Scraped. Rubbed. But all with an exquisite effort to be gentle.

Had pain ever felt quite so wonderful? His touch was tempered, and his brow furrowed in concentration, his tongue ever so faintly pushing out between teeth that she noticed were absolutely perfect. As was the naked chest one small fraction of an inch from her breasts.

"Not coming off," he said.

She turned away from him, and back to the mirror. She pried at her face. A paltry little piece came loose.

"I have a sudden vision of myself standing at the altar with my sister, sporting green clumps, Jack and Jill holding back laughter, and Beth and the assembled looking sympathetic."

"We'll get it off."

There was that *we* again, and all it conjured. A life of solving problems, some small and some large, some funny and some serious, with someone you could rely on.

Who would never in a million years embarrass you with a serenade outside your window, no matter how drunk he was.

Despite the spiked punch in high school, Jay had not been a drinker then, and she suspected he still was not.

"Go lie down on the couch," he said. "We'll

lay a hot cloth over your face and try it again in a few minutes."

She should protest, of course, but it seemed unnecessarily surly, like women who did not allow doors to be held open for them. Maybe, just for once in her life, she could surrender to being looked after.

So Jolie did as he asked and he busied himself at the sink. A few minutes later, he came and perched on the edge of the couch, gently laid a very hot washcloth over her face. He pressed it down around her eyes and nose and mouth.

She could feel his fingertips on the other side of that hot cloth. It felt like an exotic massage and it was unfairly sensual.

"You don't have to do this," she protested, a little too late, and not too vehemently.

"Ah," he said, "what are fiancés for?"

"I'm sorry. It seems a lot to ask, even of a fiancé, particularly a fake one. It's the middle of the night. Except not in Italy."

"Speaking of Italy," he said, "I have a confession to make."

"You do?"

"I speak Italian."

With a name like Fletcher? Life was just unfair sometimes.

"My mom's side."

She could feel the mask melting again. "How well?" she croaked.

"Not well, but better than him." He said it in Italian, and she really thought it was very good. And amazingly sexy.

Twice now, she'd referred to his performance in Italian, thinking he couldn't understand her. "I'm embarrassed."

"Don't be. I should have told you sooner."

"Not just by what I said. But by him. By my choices, I guess."

"It's not your fault he cheated on you." Another thing she hadn't known he knew, because she hadn't known he spoke Italian. "You deserve better."

"My sister and I were just talking about that. Family patterns. My father was not given to faithfulness."

Why would she tell him *that*?

"Don't worry," he said, "I've figured out there's no such thing as the perfect family."

"Yours always seemed like it was," she said a little wistfully.

"Yeah," he said, and his expression hardened, "until it wasn't."

"I'm sorry," she said. "I don't know why I said that. I say the wrong thing sometimes. I wondered if I did it today at some point. You seemed, um, changed on the way home."

"Did I?"

"Was it about me paying for the dress?"

"No, I'm just kind of used to picking up the tab when I'm with a woman."

"If it's a date!"

"We're engaged," he reminded her. "Ask Anthony."

He obviously had not really given the payment of the dress another thought.

"So why were you so different on the way home?"

He didn't answer right away. Then he sighed.

"You make me feel things I don't want to feel," he told her softly. "You saw the perfect family. I grew up feeling it was the perfect family. I never had a doubt. Then my dad died and she fell apart. Love failed spectacularly. She became a zombie. The love of her kids and for her kids wasn't enough to bring her back."

Jolie heard, not bitterness in his voice, but excruciating pain. It made her ache for him.

"Anyway," he said gruffly, "I saw what love did to my mom. I'm not going there. Not ever."

Jolie's heart felt paralyzed again. Jay Fletcher had seen the potential for love between them?

Okay, he'd very sensibly rejected the possibility, but still…

"I'm not going there again, either," she said, firmly. "Look at the mess it brought me last time.

I haven't even finished cleaning that up yet. Obviously."

"Really?" Jay said, quietly. "Two people burned by love. We should be the safest two people in the world to be friends."

Jolie's poor face was a mess, Jay thought. The mask had hardened just like the concrete that it resembled and it did not want to let go.

Plan B—the hot cloth—softened it, somewhat, but it still took a long time for Jay to peel it off, trying so hard to be careful and not hurt her. Even with his best efforts, there was the occasional wince and whimper.

He was so aware of her nearness, her scent and her skin beneath his fingers that his whole body was tingling.

Given that they should have been the two safest people in the whole world to be friends, it was funny how this didn't feel safe at all.

Of course, he had known it wasn't safe. That's why he'd been such a jerk on the way home from Penticton, the Peach City, where he had learned to his astonishment that peach was just about his favorite color in the whole world.

Or at least when Jolie modeled it.

He wasn't sure he was ever going to be able to bite into a peach again without thinking about her.

Danger was not red, after all.

He was still a little surprised about her vehemence about paying for the dress. This was part of his world now. He had a lot of money and most people knew it. There was an expectation, particularly when he was with a woman, that he would pick up the tab.

He liked it that she didn't know. He liked it very much that she was self-reliant, but not in the way where she wouldn't let a man open the door for her.

Unless she was mad.

At the same time, he would have liked to have purchased that dress for her. After their paths were parted, maybe she would think of him when she wore it.

Would their paths part? Or would they keep in touch? His desire for self-preservation thought a separation of paths would be best.

Still, he'd made one attempt at self-preservation today, and he'd hurt her feelings doing it.

The man he had looked up to most in the entire world—his dad—would not be proud of him.

So, in the interest of being the man his father had always thought he was, Jay decided he could suck it up for a couple of days.

"You missed dinner," he told Jolie as he plucked away at her face. She'd closed her eyes. That should have been better than those brown eyes fastened on his, but with her eyes closed, he noticed the sweep of her lashes.

The curl of her hair.

The fullness of lips that he had tasted.

"Sabrina has some planned activities for tomorrow. Horseback riding."

He thought planned activities were probably very safe. The comfort of the crowd, the perimeters of the activity.

"It's so hot. I can't imagine that would be very much fun for the people or the horses," Jolie said a little dubiously.

"Fun doesn't seem to be the goal. She said it was team building." He kept his tone deliberately neutral.

"Who needs team building for a wedding?"

So glad she had said it.

"She probably organized that before she knew my parents had delayed their arrival. You know, keep everybody occupied, try to keep the friction at a minimum."

So she expected friction between her parents. Well, there was always lots of friction between Troy and Sabrina, too.

Despite the sword hidden in it at the end, had the love of his family been a gift? He hadn't allowed himself to think of it like that, but seeing what Jolie was up against, he wished she could experience what he'd had.

Instead, he thought wryly, he seemed to be experiencing what she had. Friction. As much as he thought team building was a terrible idea for a wedding, he did think a structured environment might help keep those fractious levels of awareness down.

"Are you just about done?" she asked.

He was done. He looked down at her face. It looked awful, with painful red splotches all over it.

"How does it look?"

He didn't want to be the bearer of the truth, so he went to the bathroom, found a hand mirror and held it out to her. Jolie sat up and looked at herself.

"Oh, no," she said.

He saw all her insecurities pass over her face. He remembered how her shoulders had hunched when she'd gone into the breakfast room this morning. He remembered the snide *yellow* comment. He could imagine The Four snickering at her face tomorrow. Or maybe behind her back, since he had chastised them.

He had probably not succeeded at stopping the meanness, just driving it underground.

He knew why they were mean to Jolie, totally threatened by someone who eclipsed them in every single area. With the exception of self-confidence.

He remembered his original mission, before it had gotten waylaid by a peach dress.

Hold that mirror up to her until she could see who she really was.

Be the better man, he told himself.

Which would mean what exactly?

He was afraid he might say a lot more than *grow up* to those mean girls this time. Because despite all his efforts at distance, this evening after rescuing her from Anthony and the mask, he felt closer to her than ever.

Protective.

Of her. Because he certainly couldn't protect himself and her at the same time. He was leaving himself wide-open in the way he least liked being wide-open.

Vulnerable.

Suck it up, he ordered himself again.

"What would you think if we took a miss on team building?"

Her whole damaged face lit up.

See? Vulnerable. A man could live for that look.

"The lodge has some canoes they sign out to guests. I could pack us some breakfast things and come get you first thing in the morning, before the team builders assemble for their outing. I'll send them a text just before we leave saying we've opted out. I bet an hour or two in the fresh air and those marks will completely disappear."

Plus, it wouldn't be anything like sharing the close confines of the car with her, watching the wind tangle with her hair. It wouldn't be anything like sharing a waffle with her. It wouldn't be anything like watching her try on that little slip of fabric yesterday.

It wouldn't be a hands-on encounter like tonight had unexpectedly turned into.

"Have you ever been in a canoe?" she asked him.

It was a sport his company was not involved in. He was pretty sure it involved about six feet between paddlers. It was definitely a no-contact activity. His view would be of her back for the few hours that they would be on the lake.

"No," he said, making a note to himself to take a quick internet lesson on canoeing after he left here. "But how hard can it be?"

As it turned out, it could be quite hard. Even with Jay having prepared himself with a slew of internet tutorials, he was not sure anything could ready a person for the shocking instability of a canoe.

He was suddenly glad for the life jackets for two reasons: their lifesaving capabilities might come in handy; more importantly, Jolie encased in the puffy orange marshmallow looked nothing like she had in that dress yesterday.

Her hair was sensibly tamed, clipped at her neck. Her poor welted face was in the shadow of a ball cap. Her legs looked long and lean and sunbrowned, but once she was seated, he wouldn't have to look at that particular temptation for the rest of the outing.

But even getting seated was not simple.

The canoes were tied along both sides of the dock, and he had been assigned a red one. For a no-contact sport, Jay noticed her hands were pretty tight on his as he stood on the dock and tried to keep her and the canoe steady at the same time as she lowered herself into it.

The boat rocked alarmingly as she found the seat behind her. When it had steadied, Jay handed her the breakfast things to tuck in, and for a moment it seemed all would be lost as the vessel dipped hard toward him as she reached for the items.

She laughed and the morning took on all kinds of dangers that seemed more immediate than a capsized canoe. After she'd gotten the breakfast items organized, he dared to hand her a paddle, and there was more rocking when she reached out to take it.

Finally, he released the vessel—which he already pretty thoroughly hated—from its mooring, and used his paddle to balance on the gunnels to take his place at the back of the canoe, or the stern, as the videos had called it.

He experimentally used his paddle to push off from the dock, then dipped it into the water and pulled it back.

The canoe shockingly obeyed and they moved away from the dock.

"I'll paddle this side, and you paddle that side," he called to her.

Really, once they were moving forward it seemed pretty simple as long as they sat ramrod straight on the extremely uncomfortable seats, and didn't make any sudden movements.

"Talk about team building," he muttered, as they headed out and tried to coordinate their paddles.

"Oh, but this is so romantic."

He grunted disapprovingly.

"I mean," she caught herself, "the *romance* is of the activity, not us. Look how quiet it is, the glide through the water, the morning light on the vineyards. It's wonderful."

It wasn't really. It was hard work to paddle, impossible to steer, and even breathing the wrong way made the vessel sway threateningly to and fro in the water.

He felt overly responsible for Jolie's safety. When a motorboat roared by, they nearly capsized in the wake it left behind it.

But, despite the challenges, they both got the hang of it, and were soon skimming the water and enjoying the novel view of the shoreline. At first there were houses and small businesses, a yacht club and another resort.

The road that serviced those must have ended, because soon they left development—or civilization, depending how you looked at it—behind. The lake was even more beautiful then, with its deep forested shorelines, rocky, steep outcrops, secret coves and sandy isolated beaches.

Jay relaxed. It was a bit of a workout, but it was a great way to see the shoreline. After an hour or so, they stopped in a tiny cove, resting their paddles on the gunnels and enjoying the gentle swaying of the canoe and the silence broken only by the screech of a hawk nearby. A single rustic cabin, cedar shakes grayed from weather, perched on the edge of a steep embankment. It must have only been accessible by water.

Reaching for the breakfast bun she passed him seemed treacherous as it set the temperamental vessel to rocking.

"Chew on both sides of your mouth," he warned her, "or I think we'll tip this thing right over."

"That might feel good right about now," Jolie said, a bit wistfully.

They had worked up quite a bit of a sweat paddling. Added to that, Jay noticed a sudden stifling quality to the air, the life jacket trapping heat against his body.

But he was not about to try either beaching the canoe or trying to swim off of it. He was pretty sure, from the videos he'd watched, getting back in it would be well beyond either of their skill sets.

Besides, he had not come prepared to swim, and he was pretty sure she hadn't, either.

Skinny-dipping was out of the question.

Though once a man had allowed a thought like that into his head, it could be difficult to get rid of it.

CHAPTER TWELVE

"LET'S HEAD BACK," Jay suggested, after they had finished the buns.

Jolie did not want to go back. Even though her arms and shoulders ached from the unfamiliar exertion of paddling, she was not sure she had ever had an experience as perfect as this one.

Early morning on the lake, stillness, the sharp scent of a man in the air, her and Jay totally in sync with each other.

Team building.

"We'll be really ready for a dip when we get back to Hidden Valley," he suggested.

The promise of a different experience made leaving this one a little easier!

They paddled back out to the mouth of the cove. Even before they got entirely back to the main body of the lake, it was obvious something had changed.

While in the cove, protected, they had missed the fact the wind had risen on the main body of water.

Where it had been smooth as glass less than half an hour ago, now the water was moody, and had a distinctive chop on it. In the distance, back the way they had come, toward Hidden Valley, dark clouds boiled up.

"It's unusual to see a thunderstorm this early in the day," Jay said. She heard something in his voice and glanced back at him.

She realized right away that the calm note in his voice was for her benefit. His mouth was set in a straight, determined line. Tentatively, they pushed out into the main body of the lake.

It was quickly apparent that even the most skilled canoeist would be challenged by trying to go into the wind. The water was getting rougher, the chop was pushing back on the canoe. She was soon exhausted, discouraged by their lack of headway and starting to feel scared.

When she glanced back, Jay was a picture of pure resolve. That strength she had glimpsed in his honed body last night made up for his lack of experience. The look on his face was a look a woman could hang on to.

It was the look of a man who rose to what circumstances gave him and dug deep into his reserves of courage and fortitude.

It was the look of a man who did not allow bad things to happen on his watch.

It was the look of a man who would lay down his own life to protect others.

But even Jay's willpower was no match for the mounting storm. The rough water began to form whitecaps. The lake was rolling. A rogue wave broke over the bow, soaking Jolie, but worse, sloshing water into the boat.

"There's a can there," Jay said. "Bail."

Though his tone remained calm, there was no missing the note of urgency.

She rested her paddle on the gunnels and reached back for the can. Unfortunately, in her eagerness to save the canoe from sinking, when Jolie reached for the can—rolling just out of her reach in the center of the wallowing canoe—she overbalanced the vessel. It tipped alarmingly in the stormy waters.

Horrified, she watched her paddle slip off the gunnels and into the lake. Her every instinct was to make a grab for it, but Jay's voice stopped her.

"Leave it," he commanded, wisely, since grabbing the paddle bobbing tantalizingly just out of reach would further destabilize them.

Trying to be mindful of balance, she made one more desperate effort to get to the bailing can. Her fingertips closed around the lip, and she could have cried with relief.

But there was no time for something as self-indulgent as crying.

"Bail," he yelled over the storm, and she frantically began to empty water out of the canoe. The can did not feel nearly big enough, like trying to empty a bathtub with a teaspoon, but she could see it was making a marginal difference, and redoubled her efforts.

"I'm turning back to the cove."

It was the only reasonable thing to do, particularly now that they were down to one paddle.

There was a precarious moment when the canoe was broadside to the waves.

More water sloshed in, and over her, but she ignored it, working as fast as she could to empty it back out.

Jay turned the canoe around. Obviously the paddling was easier now that they were being driven by the waves instead of against them. Still, with only one person paddling, it seemed as if it took forever to find that mouth again.

Finally, with one last powerful heave from Jay, the canoe nosed into the calmer waters of the cove, though even inside the cove the water now had a chop on it.

But the wind was broken somewhat, and Jolie was able to make some headway on the water inside the boat as no more was sloshing in over the side.

Jay, his chest heaving, his breathing hard, took a much-needed break. She could see him casting a look out onto the lake and at the sky, weighing options.

"We're going to have to wait it out, and maybe not on the water."

"You had me at not on the water," she called back to him. "I can't get onto dry land fast enough."

The first big fat drop of rain fell on them. Jay paddled them toward shore. Though she thought she'd probably had the easier of the two jobs, she was nearly limp with exhaustion.

Despite that, he called encouragement. "Nearly there. Hang in there. Good job on the bailing. Everything's okay."

She needed to look at him. It seemed to be taking a long time to get to shore. It was as if the water, itself, was trying to stop them. Despite her trepidation about doing anything to disturb the balance of the canoe, she twisted in her seat and looked at Jay.

Despite his encouraging tone, she saw the worry in his eyes. Still, he was calling the strength from her, expecting her best, and she found herself digging deep for her reserves.

The water in the cove was getting more storm-tossed by the second. The temperature seemed to be dropping rapidly. The sky had turned a menacing shade of gray.

Another fat raindrop fell. Jolie had heard the expression *the sky opened up* but she was not sure she had ever experienced it as thoroughly as in that moment. The rain poured down. They were already wet from the water sloshing in the canoe, but this was a brand-new kind of drenched.

It soaked through her ball cap and the life jacket. Her hair was wet to her scalp. Her clothes clung to her as if they were suddenly made of cold, slimy mud.

She let out a cry of pure relief when the canoe finally hit shore with a terrible grinding clatter that sounded as if it was tearing the bottom out of the vessel. She scrambled to get out. Even at this last moment, the canoe threatened to capsize. Jay leaned hard the other way to balance it, and she was finally, gratefully and gleefully, free of the canoe.

She was up to her thighs in water. But it didn't matter. Her feet were on solid ground, and it was not possible to get any wetter.

Jay vaulted out, too. He patted his shirt pocket making sure his phone was there. A lifeline. A way to let the others in the wedding party know they were okay.

He came to the front of the canoe, and jerked it from the water, scraping it across the rocky beach. She rushed to help him, but she was shaking so badly she wasn't sure she helped at all.

Finally, panting with exertion and adrenaline,

they pulled the canoe well up out of the water, which was now pounding on the shoreline. They overturned it.

She looked out toward the mouth of the cove. It was barely visible through the sheets of rain that fell.

It sank in.

They were safe. Jay had saved them both.

CHAPTER THIRTEEN

THOUGH JOLIE WAS cold and wet and shaking with exhaustion and shock, she was experiencing something far more powerful than relief.

A beautiful euphoria enveloped her.

She felt so alive. She could feel the beat of her own heart, the blood moving through her veins.

She tilted her head and took in Jay: his hair plastered to his head, the raindrops cascading down the gorgeous lines of his face, his cheekbones, his nose, his jaw.

His lips.

She had seen people, on the news and in movies, kiss the ground in relief when they had gotten off a bad flight, or been snatched from the jaws of danger and finally found themselves on safe ground.

As much as an overreaction as that might have been, she had a wild desire to do that. But watching the rain sluice down his lips made her think, why kiss the ground, when she could kiss the man who had used every ounce of his strength and intelligence, his discipline and his never-quit attitude to get them back to a place where they were safe?

He looked every inch the warrior as he stood there, his gaze fastened on the lake that had nearly taken them.

Suddenly, with clarity she had rarely experienced in her life, Jolie knew exactly what she wanted.

Shockingly, it had not changed much since she was sixteen.

She wanted Jay's lips on her lips and his hands on her body. She wanted their skin together, she wanted to know him completely, for every barrier between them to come down.

She stepped into him.

He thought she wanted only comfort, and he pulled her close—or as close as the puffy life jackets would allow.

And then he kissed the top of her head—as if she was still that innocent sixteen-year-old child—and broke the embrace.

She didn't realize how cold she was until Jay's hand closed around hers, warm, strong, solid.

"Good job," he told her.

He practically had to pull her up a steep embankment to the cottage. The front of it was on stilts, built into the sheer drop off of the cliff. But there was a well-worn path around it, and they followed that to the front entry.

An old sign hung there, so weathered they could barely make out what it said.

Soul's Rest.

"What's with the names?" Jay asked.

But she felt that *exactly*, after the punch of adrenaline fighting the lake had given her, the sturdy little structure whispered of safety and sanctuary.

And something more.

A place for her and Jay to explore every single thing it meant to be a man and a woman. Alone. Together.

Her sense of delicious elation deepened. Maybe it was from escaping the jaws of death, and maybe it was because of the lovely coincidence that they found themselves in a place with a shelter as the storm broke.

But no.

Those elements played into her bliss, certainly.

But the major cause was knowing what she wanted.

And she wanted Jay Fletcher.

A tingling sense of anticipation filled her as he tried the handle. The door wasn't locked. In fact, the latch opened easily and the door sprang open to reveal a small alcove. They finally took off the dripping life jackets.

Again, with Jay's sodden clothes clinging to him, Jolie was taken with the sense of him being pure warrior, all hard edges and honed muscle.

Except for his mouth, the place that looked soft and inviting, the place where she would draw his innate kindness and his warmth to the surface.

Didn't every woman dream of being the one that the warrior laid down his weapons for? That he took off his armor for?

The one that he showed the vulnerabilities of his heart to?

Jay seemed as totally unaware of her as she was totally engrossed in him, taking in the interior of their shelter with the assessing eyes of a warrior/rescuer.

She took it in, too. Despite the fact that it had looked abandoned from the lake, the interior of the cottage looked as if someone enjoyed the space immensely.

It was rudimentary, but cozy. There was a small main room with a faded couch and a patched easy chair, an open-shelved kitchen with a small table in it. A miniature potbellied woodstove with a crooked pipe was in the center of the room. Bookshelves held well-worn paperbacks and jigsaw puzzles and games.

The whole lake-facing wall was windows, now being rattled by the storm, raindrops sliding down the panes.

"Supplies," Jay said, going over and perusing the open shelves. "Hot chocolate. Tea. Some canned stuff."

Here she was admiring the surprising ambience of the little space—and plotting the conquer of his lips—and he was focusing on banal things.

Survival.

This was why men and women belonged together. They balanced each other.

"We won't be here long I'm sure," Jay said, "but I'll replace anything we use. You look like you need something hot. And to get out of those wet things."

Disrobing felt like the best idea, *ever*, for a woman who had just decided men and women belonged together. Needed each other. Should celebrate their differences.

"Jay," Jolie said softly, "thank you."

He looked up from the hot chocolate supplies, surprised. "For what?"

"Getting us safely off the water."

"Huh. Well, let's not forget it was my idea to be on the water in the first place."

"That's not the point," she said stubbornly. "I lost my paddle. One wrong move and that canoe could have gone over."

"We had life jackets on," he said with a lift of his shoulder. "Instead of looking at all the things that could have happened, I think we should focus on how well we worked as a team to get off the water."

She was so taken with his way of seeing it, not seeing her as weaker than him, in need of his rescue, but rather as part of the team. Equals.

"You are a great person to be with in an emergency."

He gave her a grin. "You, too."

She should have been frozen, but she felt warmed through to her soul by that casual remark.

"You should get out of those wet things now."

Somehow, she had always imagined Jay asking her to get undressed would be slightly different than this.

Had she imagined a request like that?

Only about a hundred times.

Or maybe a thousand.

Or maybe more.

When she'd been a teenager addled by thoughts of romance. She was mature now. She had life experiences.

And it didn't seem to matter.

When it came to Jay, she felt the same weakness of wanting that she had always felt. The storm hadn't caused it.

It had exposed how raw and real that wanting still was in her.

"That looks like a bedroom through that door.

Maybe go see what's in there that you could change into temporarily."

Jolie told herself sternly that she had lost command of her senses. Was she seriously plotting the seduction of Jay Fletcher?

Their close call had obviously put her into a bit of shock.

Jay had already busied himself with the business of survival. He was crumpling paper into the woodstove.

It was a good idea to get away from him for a minute, to try and gather her thoughts. She went into the side room and closed the door. It turned out to be a bedroom, the mattress rolled up on top of a double bed.

There was a dresser but when she checked it, the drawers were empty. She went and pulled the string that bound the mattress and it unrolled. The bedding was inside of it.

It was a relief to pull the soggy clothing off. She toweled off with a rough blanket, and squeezed the water from her hair.

She waited for her tumultuous thoughts to calm as feeling returned to her body. But they didn't.

When she was done, she tucked the white sheet around herself, toga style. The fabric felt like a glorious torture on skin that was singing with awareness.

Anticipation.

She opened the door and stepped out into the main room. She felt exquisitely as if she had stepped back in time. A maiden offering herself to her warrior.

Jay was crouched in front of the woodstove. He already had a pot of water on top of it. Focused intently, he fed sticks into it. He had taken off his wet shirt. The reflection of the steadily growing flame gilded his perfect skin in gold.

It only added to the sensation of a steadily growing flame inside of her.

"There's a bit of a cell phone signal," he said, without looking up from what he was doing. "I was able to send a text saying we're okay, that we've got a safe place to ride out the storm."

She said nothing.

Jay turned his head slightly and looked at her.

It was a look every woman would hope to see in the man she had chosen to be her lover. The warrior lowered his shield.

He got up slowly, straightened, took her in.

And she saw clearly in his eyes that he had, as every warrior did, a weakness.

And that it was her.

She saw in his eyes that he acknowledged he was a man, and she was a woman, and that with the slightest nudge he would allow his power to resist to be overtaken by her power to tempt.

The sensation that enveloped her was heady.

He wanted her. And she knew it. And she loved knowing it.

She knew she had been waiting for this moment for ten years, ever since he had rejected her.

"You better get out of your wet things, too," she said.

Her voice sounded soft and husky, an obvious invitation. Jay looked at her, *that* look in his eyes—masculine appreciation, surrender.

And then he seemed to catch himself. He cast his gaze wildly about the room, as if an escape route would be revealed to him if he looked hard enough. He actually looked as if he was considering the canoe and the storm!

She frowned.

A little less fight, please!

"Go get out of those wet pants," she said, again.

CHAPTER FOURTEEN

JAY GOT OUT of that small room with Jolie as fast as he could. He went into the bedroom and shut the door, resisting, just barely, an inclination to lean on it as if some force was trying to push it back open.

The door seemed like a flimsy barrier against that force.

And it was. Because the force—his foe—was not out there. She was not the foe. The enemy was inside himself.

He was in a bad spot now. She obviously had some kind of misguided hero-worship thing going on, believing he had rescued her from certain death.

And she looked astonishing with that sheet wrapped around herself, that wild tangle of wet hair cascading around her, her shoulders naked and slender and perfect. Jolie Cavaletti was like a goddess.

A goddess who had just, more or less, ordered him out of his clothes.

Ten years ago, he had said no to her. He had recognized how vulnerable she was, and that she was not ready for what she had asked him for.

Everything was changed.

They were both adults now. Jolie was a woman who knew her own mind.

And yet somethings remained the same. She was vulnerable. She'd recently lost a relationship. And then today, both of them were coming off a bad shock, a close call.

On the other hand, Jay felt as if he had used up all his strength out there on the lake. He had none left for resistance.

There was a certain euphoric feeling—being alive, having partnered with her to accomplish that—that might make it easy to accept life tempting him with its glory.

Keep a lid on it, he ordered himself.

It would be easy for things to get out of hand. He wasn't just fighting her, but the residue of elation from having cheated the lake and the storm.

And despite the fact he had minimized the danger they had just faced, the complete truth was something else. It was not uncommon to see headlines in Canada, this land of rugged extremes, that served as reminders that Mother Nature, while magnificent, also had an unforgiving and cruel side.

Just like love.

Jay sucked in a deep, steadying breath, reminding himself he had started today with a mission to be a better man.

This storm—with all its multifaceted dimensions—would pass. Anybody, including someone who had used all his strength, could muster a bit more for a short period of time. He went over to the window and looked out.

Despite the fact it looked as if it intended to rain furiously for a week—please, no—these summer storms tended to come and go very quickly.

He formulated a plan. They would dry off. They would hang their clothes by the fire. They would probably barely have time to finish the hot chocolate and it would be time to leave, to get back in that canoe and make their way down the lake.

One thing was for sure, he was not going out there wrapped in a sheet.

He looked under the bed. To his immense relief there was a trunk, and when he opened it, it had men's clothing in it.

He yanked off his pants and dried himself, deliberately not allowing himself to focus on how his skin stung, making him feel extraordinary, as if every single cell of his being was singing.

Because he knew if he focused on that, he

would know the singing was only partially because of the exhilaration of getting off the lake.

Only partially because of the rough blanket
drying his pebbled skin.

Almost entirely because of her. Jolie. The goddess who awaited him in the other room. He pulled
on the dry clothes, jeans and a faded T-shirt, and
took one more deep breath.

He felt more like a protector than he had felt
even when he was trying to get that canoe off
the water.

He made the mistake of looking at the floor,
and their puddled clothing that needed to be hung
up by the fire.

Her sodden underwear was on top.

He picked up his own things, and left hers
there. Hopefully, when he strung the clothesline
she would get the hint.

A man could only test his strength so far.

"Oh," Jolie said, when he came back into the
main room. "You found clothes."

Did she sound disappointed?

She had pulled a kitchen chair close to the
fire and was running her fingers through her
tangled hair.

He wanted to run his fingers through her hair.

She looked as if she knew exactly what she
was doing.

"Under the bed," he said with unnecessary

terseness. "I think there are things there that would fit you."

"I'm quite comfortable, thank you."

She would be. He needed to remember that. Self-defense strategy number one: Jolie was quite comfortable tormenting a man.

He rifled through some kitchen drawers until he found some twine. He focused intently on getting a clothesline hung close to the stove.

She got up and moved over to the window. Out of the corner of his eye, as he draped his soaked clothes over the line, he noticed her studying the shelves, running her fingers over some of the games there.

"Have you ever played this?" she asked, plucking a slender box from the shelf and showing it to him.

"Probably a million times, growing up. Friday was always game night. My mom loved it so much. You would have thought she was getting ready for the event of the century every week. I think she started planning what treats she was going to serve and which game we were going to play on Monday."

He had not allowed himself these kinds of memories since his dad had died. He didn't want to talk about it anymore. It felt as if he couldn't stop himself.

"Sometimes it was just our family. To be honest, I don't think my dad was a game guy. I think he enjoyed it because she enjoyed it. But lots of times there were tons of people there, my parents' friends, our friends. Even when I got older, and it should have been lame, my friends had to be at our house for game night."

He caught a look on her face. She went from a siren to a faintly wistful little girl in the blink of an eye.

"You haven't played that game?" he asked her.

"We weren't that kind of a family," she said. She slid the box back onto the shelf.

"You didn't play any games? What about at Christmas?"

"Christmas." She made a face. "Always the worst."

Christmas? The worst? "In what way?"

Jolie looked pensive, weighing how much to tell him.

"Christmas was party time," she said finally, and he felt the weight of her trust in him. "There was way too much drinking. My father, not that inhibited to begin with, lost any inhibitions he had. He loved attention from the ladies. It seems there was always a Christmas fling. My mom would be furious at first, and they'd have these dish-shattering rows, and he'd leave. But then her fury would die down, and she'd just want him back. It always seemed as if Sabrina and I were being asked to pick a side. I was Team Dad, she was Team Mom."

"That's awful," Jay said. "I can't imagine how you dealt with that."

"I escaped into books. How grateful I was to have different worlds waiting to welcome me. All I had to do was open the cover."

He suddenly remembered how she'd been in high school, the sweet little geek, absent-minded and ethereal. She'd always had a book. He remembered sometimes other kids would say she just carried them to look smart.

War and Peace.

Moby Dick.

Les Misérables.

But even before he'd done that science project with her he'd known somehow when you were smart you didn't have to *look* smart. She probably would have done anything *not* to look so smart.

Even his totally self-centered eighteen-year-old self had known Jolie found refuge in her books and her brains.

Until now, he hadn't known what she needed refuge from.

The memory of Jolie at sixteen—wary, lacking in confidence, trying to fade into the background—diffused some of what he felt when he looked at her wrapped in that sheet.

"Sadly," she said, "sometimes those books made

me long for the things I'd never experienced growing up. When Anthony came along, I convinced myself he made me so blissful. In hindsight, I adored his family that he'd found in Italy. It was loud and boisterous and big and everything I had never had. His *nonna* adored me and the feeling was mutual. I realize I did have a few tiny little doubts about him, but I just steamrollered over them, so invested in my own happy ending."

Jay was reminded, again, of the gifts his family had given him. He could not have been given a more perfect distraction from the intensity that was leaping up between he and Jolie. Despite her admission she was—or had been—a woman in search of a happy ending, he needed to put self-protection aside.

He could be a better man. He went and took the game off the shelf.

"Go get your wet stuff," he suggested, "and hang them up on the line. I'll set up the game and get hot chocolate ready."

For a brief moment, she looked as if she had another plan, but then her gaze went to the game, and he saw that wistful little girl again. She disappeared into the bedroom without a word.

He didn't even watch her put those delicate things on the line next to his as he finished preparing their hot chocolate then set up the game. He scowled down at the board, trying to remember where everything went, and what the rules were.

A good thing to remember: what the rules were.

After she was done hanging her things, she came and settled down in a chair, and he took the one facing her.

Her whole demeanor, as he explained the game to her, took him back to her scholarly intensity in high school.

Thank goodness.

The game, called Combustion, was a combination of luck and strategy. Her brilliance was quickly apparent in how fast she caught on to the strategy part of it.

The game was one of those back-and-forth ones, where it looked as if one person was going to win but then, just before that happened, the opposing player could send them back to the beginning to start all over again.

She was intensely competitive, and so was he.

She chortled gleefully when she "killed" him and he had to start over. She cried out with outrage when he did the same to her.

Seeing her childish delight in the game initially did exactly as Jay had hoped and reduced his awareness of the fact she was certainly not sixteen anymore and she was dressed only in a sheet.

But as time went on, he noticed her hair was drying, and as it dried, these crazy corkscrew curls leaped around her.

And she threw herself more enthusiastically into the game, the sheet proved flimsy, indeed. It kept slipping and moving and she was so engrossed in the game she didn't notice.

Either that or she was so diabolically invested in winning she was distracting him on purpose with her malfunctioning wardrobe.

He looked, hopefully, out the window. The rain sluiced down, unabated.

"I win!" Jolie cried.

He saw the pure happiness on her face. Maybe he wasn't so sorry the rain wasn't stopping, after all.

"Want to go again?" she asked.

Jolie won the game three times in a row. She eyed Jay with sudden suspicion.

"Are you letting me win?"

"I'm not that chivalrous."

But she suspected that he was, indeed, that chivalrous. Suddenly, she lost interest in the game. She was with the man she had wanted to be with since she was sixteen years old. There might never be another opportunity like this one in her entire life.

"Jay," she said, "I'm not a kid anymore."

"Thanks," he said dryly, "gleeful winning of games aside, the slipping sheet already let me know that."

She glanced down. She was showing quite a bit more than she thought she was. She was going to adjust the sheet, but then decided against it.

"We were playing for a kiss," she told him.

"No, we weren't!"

"Jay," she said, "I don't know how to be any more direct."

"Look," he said, "you're just breaking up with your fiancé, and our near miss on the water seems to have left you with an exaggerated sense of my heroism."

She actually laughed at that, and he looked annoyed.

"Who told you that you got to make all the rules?" she asked him quietly. "I know you're an old-fashioned guy who likes to hold open doors and all that, but I know what I want. I think I know what you want, too."

"I doubt that," he sputtered.

"Let's find out."

And then, before she lost her nerve, she got up from her place at the table, crossed over to him and wiggled her way onto his lap.

He could have gotten up. He could have pushed her away. But he didn't.

She twined her arms around his neck. The sheet slipped a little more.

He wasn't exactly participating, but he wasn't exactly withdrawing, either.

Experimentally, she touched the puffiest part of his bottom lip with her fingertip.

"If it's not what you want," she whispered, "tell me."

He didn't say a word.

So she leaned in yet closer and touched the place on his lip where her fingertip had been with the faintest flick of her tongue.

She stopped, looked at him. He returned her gaze. He still didn't say a word.

Then Jolie caressed his bottom lip with her top lip, nuzzling, a touch as light as a butterfly wing.

It wasn't like when she had kissed him for Anthony's benefit. It wasn't like that at all. It was more like her heart had waited for this moment all these years, and it sighed in recognition as she deepened the kiss.

Everything about her said, without having to say a single word, *I know you.*

His resistance collapsed when she scraped her lips lightly, back and forth, over his. With a groan of surrender, he caught her to him, bracketed her face with his hands and returned her kiss.

With hunger.

And passion.

With curiosity.

And satisfaction.

And ultimately, with certainty.

His hands moved to her hair, catching in it, stroking it, untangling it. Somehow the sheet slipped between them, and he was balancing her with one arm and tearing off his shirt with the other.

So that they could have this.

Full contact. Full sensation. Full awareness.

Heated skin on heated skin.

His eyes dark with need, his gaze swept her own, looking for permission, for affirmation. He found both, and his head dropped over her breast.

Thunder rolled outside, and the rain slashed the window. Lightning split the sky.

The power of the storm was nothing compared to what was unfolding between them.

CHAPTER FIFTEEN

WITHOUT MOVING JOLIE from his lap, Jay stood up. She managed to free her legs from the tangle of the sheet and tuck them around the hard strength of his hips.

She marveled at the ease with which he carried her. There was no pause in his lips laying claim to hers. He tasted her neck and ears and her cheeks as he carried her through to the bedroom, the sheet caught between them, and dragging on the floor.

He dropped her gently down onto the bed, pulled the tangle of the sheet completely away from her and paused for a moment, something like reverence darkening his eyes. They looked, suddenly, more black than green.

Then Jay dispensed with his jeans in a flash faster than lightning and came onto the bed. He was poised above her, holding his weight off of her with his elbows, anointing her with kisses and flicks of his tongue.

He was extra gentle with where her face was

still splotched from the mask. Still, it felt as if he might be leaving marks of his own, as he trailed fire across her skin.

Jay was an exquisite lover. He was possessive and tender, but there was also no mistaking the leashed masculine strength in every touch of his hands and his lips. He seemed determined to leave no inch of her unexplored, her belly, her breasts, her neck, the bottoms of her feet.

Without saying a single word, his breath on her skin said hello to each muscle, each limb, each eye, each toe. His lips welcomed her and celebrated this new way of knowing each other.

She could feel need building in her, screaming along her nerve endings, but he would not give in.

He tantalized.

He took her to the edge of desire, until she was nearly sobbing with wanting him, and then inched back, began the dance of knowing her all over again.

Only when both of them were quaking with need, slick with sweat, so desperate that it felt as if death were near, did he combine conquest and surrender.

With an exquisite mix that was part the fury of the storm, and part the tenderness of souls who had retreated from each other for far, far too long, they came together.

Jolie and Jay joined in that exquisite and ancient dance that the very universe felt as if it had been born out of. They came together and then fell apart.

Like a shooting star falls apart, a projectile penetrating a dark sky and then exploding, thousands of sparks of light falling, falling, falling back to Earth.

Winking out, one at a time.

"Jolie," he whispered her name against her throat, and then even softer, "Jolie."

Jay saying her name like that, as if it was a blessing, made her seduction of him feel so right.

Her boldness rewarded.

In those moments after, had Jay shown the slightest awkwardness, had there been even a moment's regret in his eyes, she might have questioned what had just happened between them, and how it had happened.

Her pushing against his reluctance.

But there was none of that.

Instead, he propped pillows up against the headboard, pulled that sheet up around them, invited her into the circle of his arms.

They talked. They talked about his business, and about her work. They talked about life in Rome and life in Toronto. They talked about their families and shared memories from their childhoods, some funny, some poignant.

There was a sense that they could talk forever, never run out of things to say.

And then, as quickly as the storm had come up, it was gone. The sun came out and streamed across their bodies, made them freshly aware of each other. It felt as if it was her turn, this time, to explore and celebrate every single thing that made up Jay.

After, when she lamented the lack of running water in the cabin, he laughed, and gestured to the window. "Look at our bathtub."

So, wrapped in sheets they made their way down the rocky pathway to the water's edge.

He dropped his sheet first and dove cleanly into the water.

They played. They swam and splashed, and chased each other, until they were exhausted from both laughter and exertion.

Standing up to their waists in the water, Jay pulled her to him and cupped the cold, pure lake water in his hands, and poured it over her hair, worked it through with tender fingertips. And then he did the very same to the rest of her body, until she had never felt quite so clean in her entire life.

It was her turn, and he knelt in the water, so she could easily reach his hair.

But she had hardly begun when he leaped back to his feet.

"What?"

"I hear a motor. A boat is coming."

At first she didn't hear what he did, but then there was no mistaking it. Laughing like naughty children, they rewrapped themselves in sheets and scrambled up the trail to the cabin. She was glad they had retreated, because the boat pulled into their cove and cut the engine, drifting in toward where they had been playing naked moments before.

Both of them began pulling on the clothes that hung on the line, still faintly damp, terribly crusty and uncomfortable.

"Hell. It's Troy," Jay said. "He's probably coming to check on us."

He looked around and found his phone. He wagged it at her. "They've been texting for hours. This last one says he's coming in a boat. They'll bring us back."

She realized, stunned, that their moment was over as quickly as the storm.

"I'll go tell him we'll take the canoe back."

"Oh," she said, "I'm not sure I want to. Get back in the canoe."

"I think it's like falling off a horse, Jolie. You get right back on."

"There's only one paddle," she said, desperate to not get back in that tippy little vessel with all its potential for sudden death.

"I saw some under the cabin. We'll make sure we return everything we've borrowed."

"I'm scared," she said.

He laughed. He actually threw back his head and laughed. "No, you're not, Jolie. You're the boldest, bravest woman I've ever met."

It occurred to her you could become the things that someone else believed about you.

Maybe she had done that her whole life, but in the reverse of this. Becoming less than she was, instead of more.

"The thing about fear," Jay said softly, "is that once you've let it take hold, it doesn't want to let go. It takes on a life of its own. It grows and grows."

"Okay," she said, "go tell him we'll canoe back."

After he left, she contemplated the simple courage he was asking of her, that he saw in her, and that he was calling into existence.

This is what love did, then, it made you bigger, stronger, better than you had been before.

It didn't rip you to shreds one little nip at a time.

Love?

She wasn't in love with Jay just because she had slept with him. It would be unbelievably naive to think that.

He had made it clear from the beginning that he did not trust love.

Why would she? After seeing her parents?

After catching a man she had trusted with her whole heart stepping out on her?

So she would not call it love.

And yet there was no denying the feeling in her heart—even if she left it unnamed—filled her with a deep sense of bliss.

Not quite like anything else she had ever known.

They did canoe back to the lodge. It was not easy getting back in the canoe. In fact, it was terrifying.

And yet, conquering that terror filled her with a sense of her own ability to overcome adversity.

She had Jay to thank for that. The best man pulling the very best from her.

They arrived at the resort to a hero's welcome. The entire bridal party were waiting for them on the shore.

After the stillness and solitude of the cabin, this was a bit of a shock, and not in a good way.

After the intensity of their togetherness, being pulled into the center of a crowd, with everyone asking questions, and doling out hugs and backslaps, Jolie yearned to get back in the canoe, paddle through the stillness of the lake, just *be* with him.

She caught Jay's eye.

He winked at her.

And she saw the bond between them survived.

"Anthony left," her sister told her, with barely a hello.

Jolie felt a certain indifference to whether Anthony had left or not. She and Jay's lovemaking felt as if it had put a shield around her that others—even her ex—could not get through.

Sabrina took her arms and guided her up toward the resort. "And Mom and Dad have arrived."

Jolie hesitated. "How are they?"

"So worried about you!"

"That's not what I meant."

"Oh. How *are* they? Like lovebirds. He's doting on her. I should know better, but I actually wonder if they've worked it out this time."

The names of these cabins. Heart's Refuge and Lovers' Retreat. Maybe this was a magical place.

Where Troy and Sabrina were going to get it right.

Where her mother and father were going to figure it all out, finally.

And where love had touched her.

There was that word again. But why not? It seemed as if it was in the air.

"They were so worried about you, Jolie. I have to take you to them right away. And then a dress arrived that I ordered online. You should try it."

Jolie pulled away from her sister's arm. Once,

she might have liked this, being at the center instead of on the outside.

But she had been canoeing since her very sexy rinse in the lake, and there had been no soap or shampoo involved in that.

Plus, she needed to gather herself before a family reunion.

"I have to have a shower and change clothes."

"Okay," Sabrina said, "but could you be quick about it? Oh, my gosh, Jolie, we only have one full day left before the wedding. It suddenly feels as if there's way too much to do and not enough time to do it."

Jolie wasn't sure about the way-too-much-to-do part, but it did feel, suddenly, as if there was not enough time.

"A quick shower," she promised her sister.

She went to her cabin, stripped off her clothes and got under the hot steamy jets, lifting her face to them. Her body felt delightfully different, as if she was aware of the sensuality of being alive in ways she had never been before. The steam, the hot water hitting her body, the way the pebbled shower tray felt on her feet all held sensations Jolie had not been aware of before.

Though her eyes were closed, the air changed ever so slightly, a breath of cold air touched her.

It was the shower curtain being pulled back.

She didn't have to open her eyes to know. Her

heart recognized that his presence had its own feel to it.

Wordlessly, he got in behind her, nuzzled the silky wetness of her neck, before reaching past her for the soap. She realized, as much as she had been aware of sensation before Jay had gotten into the shower with her, it had not been sensual.

This was sensual. His hands, slippery with soap, exploring her entire body, mapping it, marking it, with soap and then with kisses when the soap was rinsed free.

He replaced the soap, and reached by her, this time for the shampoo. He added some to his cupped palm, and then worked it into her hair, his fingertips strong, sure, familiar.

Still, without a word, when the shampoo had rinsed free, and he had wrung her hair out between his hands, and finger-combed the tangles, he lifted her into his arms and put her wet body on the bed.

Wet bodies, it turned out, were twice as erotic as dry bodies.

"Now I have to shower again," she told him, pretending to complain after, gazing up at him, her palm grazing his chin.

He nipped her fingers. "I know," he said. "Isn't that great? It's your turn."

And so she had her turn, soaping him, getting to know every inch of his beautiful body, her hands sliding over hard and soft surfaces, in and out of his ears, the dip at his collarbone, his belly button.

It was shockingly exciting even before the real shock of the water running cold before she was finished. Jay shoved her gently out of the cold spray, finished washing off the soap himself and then came out and they dried each other off.

And that was how the rest of the day, and the hours before the wedding the next day, unfolded.

On the surface, Jolie sailed through her bridesmaid's duties. She met with her parents, and tried on the new dress, which was neither as ugly as the first one, nor as sexy as the second one. It was a nice bland dress that could not dampen down the feeling she carried inside her.

That she had a secret.

The secret was that she was not bland.

The secret was that she was a heated lover.

Jolie and Jay stole kisses behind the arbor they had been assigned to sew flowers onto. He was waiting for her along the pathway to the lodge for the rehearsal dinner, pulled her into the trees with him and covered her with kisses.

And then they sat, one of them on one side of the groom, and one on the other side of the bride, not making eye contact, nursing their secret.

She suspected everyone had assumed their relationship was fake, designed to dissuade Anthony.

Now that nothing about what they were doing together felt fake—it felt, in fact, like the realest thing that had ever happened to her—Jolie had a desire to keep it under wraps.

To not indulge in public shows of affection, to not exchange endearments, to not convince anyone anything was going on.

Ironically, it was the reverse of what she had wanted when she had first asked Jay to pretend he was her fiancé.

Impossibly, that was only a few days ago. The changes between them made it feel as if that arrangement had happened in a separate lifetime.

What was really going on now was so new it felt fragile, like it could be easily broken by a wrong move.

She did not want it scrutinized by her sister's cynical friends.

She did not want them weighing in behind her back on the way she and Jay looked at each other and touched each other and listened to each other.

What had started out as so public now felt intensely private.

You did not put the sacred on display.

CHAPTER SIXTEEN

JOLIE DID NOT consider herself a wedding person. She had not even really felt as if she was one when she had been planning her own wedding to Anthony.

Despite her enjoyment of the gown she had chosen, planning her own wedding had felt like a duty rather than a joy, something she had to get through in order to get to the next stage of her adult life, which was supposed to have been marriage.

Most of the weddings she had been to just seemed way too much like a stage set, too much about the wedding and not enough about the marriage.

There always seemed to be quite a bit of behind-the-scenes drama with a major wedding event.

Her sister's wedding, with that initial hysteria over the dresses, had held every promise of being the same.

A hysterical bride demanding perfection from an imperfect world.

And yet, as Saturday unfolded, it was so evident her sister's wedding had been pulled back from that bad start.

Jolie gave most of the credit for this to her soon-to-be brother-in-law-for-the-second-time. Troy was just one of those decent, down-to-earth guys. He indulged a certain amount of Sabrina's histrionics, but also wasn't scared to let her know when he'd had enough, or she was going over the top.

Jolie could understand, when she saw Troy and Jay together, why they were such good friends.

They were a type.

Strong.

Reliable.

Hardworking.

And underneath all that—or maybe even because of all that—was a kind of hum of understated sexiness.

But she did have to give some credit to Sabrina as well. The destination wedding had been a good idea. The Hidden Valley setting seemed to invoke calm. The team building exercise with the horses seemed to have succeeded in deepening the relationships of everyone involved.

And though she and Jay had not been part of the team, the canoeing expedition gone so wrong had brought them into the fold and seemed to have strengthened ties within the party.

Everybody seemed aware that it could have

been a much different day today if Jolie and Jay had not got off the lake.

Her parents were on their best behavior. She'd had a chance to talk to her father, and he had told her he was a new man because of a twelve-step program he'd found that dealt with sex addiction.

She hadn't really known much about it, and certainly didn't want to know that about her father. Addicted to sex? Yuck!

But, on the other hand, now that she'd had several encounters of the intimate kind with Jay, she could understand why it could be addictive. Maybe she even had to watch out for that particular weakness in herself!

She didn't really want any of the details of her father's transgressions, and he thankfully did not volunteer them.

Instead, for the first time she could ever remember, he took responsibility for the pain he had brought to the family dynamic.

"I know I caused you all a great deal of suffering. I know I'm the reason you live in Italy," he said contritely, "as far from the chaos as you can get."

"You know, Dad, that might have been my original motivation in going there, but I genuinely love it now. I love my job. I have a sense of purpose and community. Maybe instead of seeing it as you driving me there to get away from you,

you could see it as it driving me there to where I was always meant to be. Don't you think life has a way of taking us where we're meant to be?"

Would she have believed that quite so completely before her reunion with Jay?

"Ah, Jolie, always my favorite," he said in Italian.

"Don't tell Sabrina," she whispered.

"That's why I said it in Italian."

They laughed together.

"I like your new beau," he said. "I was never that taken with Anthony."

"You never said anything!"

"I felt I lost my right to comment on such things when I had hardly set an example myself."

"What things?"

"You know. His wandering eye."

"You *knew* that?"

"I only met him once. That time I came to visit you in Rome. I just noticed he always seemed to be searching beyond you."

"Why didn't you say something?"

"I didn't know how. But I like the new beau."

She blushed. "*Beau* might be a little too strong."

"Not the way he's looking at you. Now, there's a man who has eyes for only one woman."

"Don't keep talking about him as if he's a stranger. It's Jay Fletcher, from high school."

Her father looked at her quizzically. "A little more than that, wouldn't you say?"

"You mean his sporting goods company?"

His father gave her another look. "Yes," he said, "that's what I mean."

The day that unfolded just had such a nice feeling. Everyone was relaxed and getting along.

Even Jack and Jill and Beth seemed to have left their hard edges behind them. They actually said really nice things about her hair and makeup and the new dress as they all helped each other, and Sabrina, get ready for the wedding.

It felt to Jolie as if she had finally been accepted—possibly by virtue of the fact they had contemplated losing both her and Jay to that storm.

There was a bit of anxiety when the much-anticipated Chantelle was late, but she finally arrived, breathless, saying she had taken a wrong turn out of Penticton. Jolie was not sure what she had been expecting, but the famous Chantelle was tiny, dwarfed by the multitude of cameras she carried. She was wearing a somewhat dressy form of army fatigues, and peered at them all through huge glasses with colorful frames.

She managed to get a few shots of them getting ready.

"Pretend I'm not here," she said with stern annoyance to Jack and Jill when they started posing for her.

And then it was time.

To the strains of the very traditional "Wedding March" by Felix Mendelssohn, the bridesmaids exited the main lodge, one at a time, slow stepping across the lawns to where the seating and an arbor had been set up by the shores of the lake.

The lake was placid today, mirrorlike, reflecting the vineyards and orchards and the spectacular houses and humble cottages that surrounded it.

The bridesmaids moved down the outdoor aisle, past the guests, the women in their beautiful summer dresses and sandals and hats, the men in light trousers and button-up sports shirts.

The groom and his groomsmen were waiting on a slightly raised dais under the arbor. Jolie only allowed herself to look at Jay briefly.

The groomsmen were beautifully dressed, in gray slacks, crisp white shirts, suspenders and bow ties.

Everything that Jay and Jolie were to each other was reflected in the deep way that he returned her brief look, the upward quirk of that mouth she had tasted over and over again, so intimately.

He gestured subtly to her dress and shook his head, *not you.*

She did the same thing for his bow tie. Even

with all these people watching and a wedding about to get under way, she was aware of how the two of them could close out the world.

She reminded herself it was her sister's day, and the looks and wordless communication she and Jay were exchanging felt as if they could steal the very sun out of the sky.

She turned her attention to Sabrina, who was coming down the grassy aisle now, one arm in her mother's and one in her father's.

Jolie realized she needn't have worried about her and Jay stealing the sun. Not today. Her sister was absolutely radiant in a summer gown, constructed of white lace and smoke and magic.

She had eyes for no one but Troy.

When Jolie glanced at Troy, she saw him—that powerful down-to-earth guy—brush a tear from his eye.

And somehow she just knew it was going to be okay this time.

Her mother and father each kissed Sabrina on a cheek and clasped hands, glanced at each other and went to their seats.

It felt as if maybe they were going to be okay, too.

In fact, here at her sister's beautiful summer wedding, with the sun shining and the birds singing, with love sparkling in the air, Jolie felt something she had rarely allowed herself to feel.

As if everything was going to be okay.

The ceremony, and the signing of the register, and the bride and groom's first kiss—extended version—proved her right. Everything went off seamlessly and she felt herself surrendering to the pure fun of the day.

Chantelle was nothing short of amazing. A few days ago, Jolie might have felt awkward posing, especially for some of the more artsy shots, but she just brought that new bolder her to it all. She noticed Jay, too, had given himself over to the day.

Making other people happy, she decided, looking at her glowing sister, was a good way to make yourself happy.

It was something that she didn't think Jack and Jill would ever learn. Instead of making the photo sensation about the bride, they vied shamelessly for Chantelle's attention.

"I think we've got a lot of good photos," Chantelle finally said, clicking through the display screen on her camera.

"If you ever want to do some modeling work," she said, and Jack and Jill nearly fell over themselves to get the card she was holding out. But she ignored them, marched passed them and handed the card to the astonished Jolie.

"Look at this photo," she said, showing it to Jolie.

Jolie looked at the woman in the photo Chantelle was showing her and almost didn't recognize herself. The woman in the photo was laughing, carefree, confident.

Jolie realized it wasn't her, so much that Chantelle had recognized as the light that was shining from her. A woman who had come into herself, completely and passionately.

She was aware of Jack and Jill also pressed close, both looking at the photo.

"I could get you a job in the industry—" Chantelle snapped her fingers "—like that."

"What industry?" Jolie asked, baffled.

"Ad campaigns, sports magazines, runway work."

"I can't even imagine," Jolie said, diplomatic enough not to finish with, *a life that shallow and dull*.

"Oh, for heaven's sake," Jill said, clearly peeved, "she's a doctor, not a model."

"A doctor," Chantelle breathed. "That explains it. The depth in your eyes. The intelligence in your face. I think the days of the too-thin vapid blonde are done in the industry, and good riddance."

Jack gasped as though she'd been stabbed.

Jolie became aware of Jay standing with them, looking down at the photo that Chantelle was showing. She glanced up at him.

A tiny, knowing smile was tickling the gorgeous line of his lips.

"I saw you first," he murmured in her ear.

It was so true. He had *seen* her first. He had drawn to the surface every single thing that Chantelle had caught with this photo. He had made her alive, and that life force shimmered in her, in a way the camera had captured.

After photos, there was a cocktail hour on the very deck where she had first sat, enveloped in that horrid dress.

She remembered that she had imagined just this: people going in and out the doors, laughter, glasses clinking.

She and Jay finally dared to stand side by side, unnoticed in all the activity.

"As far as weddings go," Jolie told him, and could hear the contentment in her own voice, "this one has been pretty peachy." He handed her a glass of wine.

"To peaches," he said and they tapped glasses. "I actually had this idea about peaches," he said. He lowered his voice to a growl, and spoke the words into her ear only.

She reared back from him, trying not to choke on wine.

He smiled wickedly, and raised an eyebrow at her.

"Jay, I'm leaving tomorrow," she said.

"What? Why didn't you mention that before?"

"I don't know. It just never came up." Their moments had engrossed her so completely that she had not looked toward that thing that never worked out for her, anyway.

The future.

"Aren't you?" she asked him, "Leaving tomorrow?"

"That was my original plan, but I seem to have taken a detour. I could be a little flexible," he said. "Can you?"

"Maybe a teensy bit."

"I'm not ready to let you go." This was growled in her ear, the same way as his naughty suggestion with the peaches had been.

That declaration and the wedding behind them suddenly made it feel okay to be publicly a couple for the first time since Anthony had left.

His hand found hers. He led her to the deck railing, and put his arm around her. She leaned her head on his shoulder as the sun went down.

The wedding feast had been set up in that grand ballroom. Jolie and Jay had not been seated together. Jay was on the groom's side of the table, she was beside Sabrina, but even so, dinner was fabulous, as were the speeches and toasts. She and Jay came together again when the dancing began.

Finally, it felt okay to be them.

It was dark now. The tables were removed from the ballroom and the doors were thrown open between the outdoor space and the indoor one, making a huge dance floor. Thousands of fairy lights illuminated both spaces.

Sabrina danced with Troy. And then they broke away from each other, and she danced with Dad and he danced with their mom.

The formalities of the order of who everyone was supposed to be dancing with seemed to Jolie to go on endlessly.

But finally, Jolie and Jay were together, dancing for the first time since the senior prom night when she had propositioned him.

She realized she was so thankful he'd said no that night. She had not been ready. And it was possible it would have ruined *this*.

Had he said yes it was quite possible what would have happened between them would have overshadowed everything, forever. Because the things he had said to her that night were right.

She had been too young.

She had not been ready.

She had been about to get herself into trouble.

Yes might have felt good at the time, but so, so bad later. He'd only been eighteen. How had he known?

Or had he been guided by a force larger than

himself? That let him know taking that opportunity that night might remove the opportunity for a future one.

It was partly because of that long-ago no, that when they danced together, his presence invited her to be herself.

That had never been an easy thing for her.

Letting go.

CHAPTER SEVENTEEN

No, LETTING GO had never come easily to Jolie.
And yet right now, dancing with Jay, it felt as if
it was the easiest thing in the world.

She was not sure she had felt this good since
she was sixteen, drunk on a punch she had been
unaware was spiked.

She'd had very little to drink tonight, but she
felt intoxicated, nonetheless.

They danced until they were breathless. They
danced as if there was no one else on that deck
that was canopied with stars. They danced in celebration of all the ways they had come to know
each other.

When their feet started to hurt, they kicked off
their shoes and danced some more.

He drew from Jolie her confidence.

Her sexiness.

Her certainty in herself as a woman that she
had never felt with anyone but him. Even when
she was sixteen.

She never wanted this magical evening to end.

But then Jay was called away by Troy for some-thing, he kissed Jolie regretfully and departed. Breathless, she left the deck, and stood there in the darkness drinking in the stars.

"Hey, sis."

"You startled me," Jolie said, seeing Sabrina standing there, with a wineglass in her hand, al-most hidden by shrubs. "What are you doing?"

"Oh, just having a moment."

"The stars are gorgeous tonight."

"What is going on between you and Jay?" Sa-brina asked. "We could both be brides! You're radiant. Chantelle certainly saw it. Those photos are probably going to be all about you."

It was said without any kind of edge at all. Completely gone was the woman who had told her there was only to be one star of this show.

Jolie lifted a shoulder, not wanting to get into it right now.

The silence was comfortable between them for a few moments, and then Sabrina broke it.

"I'm sorry. About the first night. Making such a fuss over the dress."

"It doesn't matter now. It all worked out. This one is great."

"I've been a bit temperamental lately."

"It's a big event to plan," Jolie said.

"That's not it. Nobody knows this yet, but I'm pregnant."

Jolie felt the shock of that announcement ripple through her. She glanced at the glass in her sister's hand.

"It's sparkling juice," Sabrina said.

So that first night, the juice had been for Sabrina, not her. How often, Jolie wondered, had she been overly sensitive and made it about herself when it wasn't?

"Does Troy know?"

"Of course Troy knows," Sabrina said, insulted.

"It's just that you said nobody—"

"Oh! Do you always have to be so literal?"

Her sister loved to use the expression *literally.* This was the first time in Jolie's memory she'd actually used it correctly.

"Couldn't you just say you're happy for us?" her sister snapped. Apparently, their truce was over, because Sabrina gathered up her dress and lifted her chin. "It's half an hour from midnight. Could you go to the kitchen and check that the midnight snack is on time?"

Then she marched away with her nose in the air.

Jolie realized she still hadn't congratulated her sister. It just seemed there were too many questions, and that it might not be appropriate to ask them under their current circumstances.

For instance, was it an accident? Because Sabrina had told her Troy didn't want to have a baby.

Had her sister planned it? Like a trap? Is that why she was so defensive?

If it was true, if Sabrina had trapped Troy into this second marriage, wasn't it just a variation on the theme from their childhood?

A way of begging someone to love you?

The magic seemed to be draining from the evening as Jolie made her way to the kitchen as her sister had asked.

Her sister was pregnant.

And then another thought followed on the heels of that one.

What if *she* was pregnant? She'd stopped using birth control when she and Anthony had split. Swearing off men had meant her chances of a pregnancy were zero, after all.

She'd been so swept away by Jay that she hadn't even considered that.

No, that wasn't quite true. She'd swept Jay away, not the other way around. It was so unlike her not to think things all the way through. All right, Jay also seemed to have been swept away, not asking any of the usual questions, but ultimately the responsibility felt as if it was hers.

Certainly, protecting oneself from pregnancy would be part of that equation.

Who was she to sit in judgment of her sister?

She looked at her watch. It was, as her sister had pointed out, nearly midnight. It seemed impossible that time had gone so fast. The evening—the whole day, really—had evaporated.

But she could feel something shifting. Reality poking at the edges of her consciousness.

Wasn't this where the fairy tale ended? Where Cinderella's bubble burst? When she lost her glass slipper, the mice turned into coachmen and the coach turned into a pumpkin? She went back to her old life of being the family scapegoat?

Now, where had that thought come from, like a cloud drifting across a perfect day?

She found the long dark hallway that led to the kitchen. There was a little alcove off of it, and smoke drifted out.

And then a familiar laugh.

Jack and Jill.

Still sneaking cigarettes, as if they were teenagers hiding behind the bus garage at the high school.

Jolie went to move by the alcove when Jill's voice stopped her.

"Omg, what do you think of Jay and Jolie together?"

"Obviously, they were just pretending for Anthony."

"Well, he's gone, and they're still together."

"Are they together, or she can't let go of the pretense, and she's throwing herself at him?"

"I think Chantelle gushing over her gave her a swollen head."

"I bet she asked her to say those things. To play a little prank on us."

"Or maybe Jay did! He's been quite defensive of her from day one. He seems to want to play white knight for her."

Triumphant snickers.

Maybe slightly drunken snickers, which didn't make it any less hurtful.

"No matter what the stupid photographer said, she's punching above her weight, that's for sure."

What did that mean?

"I mean she's not the little wallflower she once was, but I don't think being a doctor and living in Italy makes her Jay Fletcher material. I mean even if one photo did give Chantelle pause, Jay is one of the richest men in the world. I heard he has a private jet waiting for him in Kelowna."

"He dated Sophia Binal for a while."

"The singer? He did not!"

"He did. I'll show you on my phone."

"Wow," Jack said a moment later.

Jay was one of the richest men in the world? What? He'd dated one of the most famous and beautiful women in the world?

She remembered her father looking at her oddly when she said Jay had a sporting goods company.

She remembered him paying for that dress as if it was nothing.

Because to him, had it been nothing?

Jolie turned hastily, determined to find a different way to the kitchen to order the evening snack.

But when she passed the bathroom where she had first tried on that peach monstrosity, she couldn't resist ducking in. It was empty, but for further privacy, she found a stall and locked the door.

She did what she had not allowed herself to do in the ten years since she had left Canada. She used her phone and she looked up Jay Fletcher on the internet.

Jay was rich, all right.

He was billionaire rich.

And Sophie Binal wasn't the only spectacularly rich and famous woman he'd had on his arm in the past ten years, either.

While she was there looking things up, she searched what *punching above your weight* meant. It might have been common in Canada, but she didn't recall ever hearing it in Italy. It was a boxing term. It meant you had entered the wrong category and were probably about to get smashed to bits by a superior opponent.

Jack and Jill had obviously meant she didn't have a hope.

Jolie got up, put away her phone and tried to compose herself.

In the kitchen, she asked for the snack, just as Sabrina had requested. When she came back out, the alcove was empty, and she sat down on an upholstered bench, even if it did smell of smoke in there.

Oddly, she did not feel diminished by the remarks she had overheard.

Jack and Jill were simply horrible people. Their opinions meant nothing to her.

She felt as if the few days of being Jay's lover had given her the truest sense of who she really was that she had ever experienced.

And so, while not diminished, Jolie still felt a need to be analytical.

It was time to put emotion—that most unreliable of forces—aside and allow herself to be guided by the facts. Which were: She had been the aggressor. She had seduced Jay.

There was new evidence that sexual addiction ran in the family. Maybe she was in the first stages of that.

She was on the rebound, as Jay had pointed out when he had tried to resist her efforts.

She had been filled with survivor's euphoria when she had made her move.

She had been bonded to the man she perceived as saving her life.

She had not taken proper precautions and there was a remote possibility of pregnancy.

And lastly, though Jay had had many opportunities, he had never revealed the full truth about himself to her.

He was the kind of man women deliberately tried to trap.

Which brought up Sabrina's news.

It all felt like too much. Sabrina's surprise pregnancy, her mother and father's reconciliation, Jolie's awareness of family patterns.

Where did her new love affair fit into all of this?

Jolie suddenly *needed* to be home. Italy was home, and there was a reason for that. It was far away from all this chaos and emotion and family drama.

She needed to ground herself, to be surrounded by her things, her books and her flowers, her cozy tiny apartment, her fulfilling, satisfying work.

She needed to be away from Jay—how could she ever think straight around him?—in order to analyze this situation correctly.

Maybe she was addicted to him, already. Because she knew if she went back out onto that deck and danced with him one more time, she would be completely under the powerful sway of the forces between them.

She would never be able to draw a logical conclusion.

Just as she had that final thought, the clock struck twelve.

It was a confirmation to her that all fairy tales come to an end. It was good to leave fantasies on a high note, before the reality set in.

Part of her insisted on pointing out the clock striking midnight was not the end of the fairy tale. There was still the part about the prince finding the glass slipper, tracking down Cinderella, making his declaration of love.

Jolie sighed.

Wasn't that what she really wanted? To know what had transpired between her and Jay hadn't been just because she'd seduced him?

Was she hoping, like in the fairy tale, he would come find her?

Of course she was! But that was a terrible, terrible weakness, to want such a thing, to believe in such a thing.

And what if she *was* pregnant? Then what?

Jolie went back to her cabin. She was not sure why she felt like a thief in the night as she quickly changed her clothes, packed up her few things, and bolted for the parking lot and her rented car.

And she was not sure why, if this was such an analytical decision, she kept having to wipe tears out of her eyes to see the dark road in front of her.

CHAPTER EIGHTEEN

"Where's Jolie?" Jay asked Sabrina.

"I'm not sure."

Did the bride seem faintly miffed about something?

"I asked her to go organize the midnight snack, but it's here now, and she's not."

Jay frowned and scanned the gathering. The dancing had ended when the clock struck midnight, and the snack had been put out. People were milling around, eating and talking. No one seemed to want to leave. It really had been a perfect day.

And yet, when the clock had struck midnight, he'd had a funny sense shiver along his spine.

The perfect day was over.

On an impulse, he checked his phone. He stared at it, not sure he was believing what he saw.

There was a text there from Jolie. It was not even to him, personally. It was a group text, to her sister and her mom and dad and him. It thanked the bride and groom for the most perfect day ever.

It said she'd had an emergency at work, and when she checked flights she'd found one that could get her back to Italy immediately.

I'll catch up with everyone later!

Breezy. Casual.

It didn't even mention him by name.

Jay felt as if he had been punched in the gut, as if the bottom was falling out of his world. Here it was, right on schedule, the sword hidden under the cloak of love.

Not that he loved her.

You didn't love a person because you'd become lovers for two days.

On the other hand, he and Jolie's history stretched back a lot longer than two days. On the other hand, he was not sure he had ever felt quite what he had felt in Jolie's arms.

Or when he was with her, setting aside the lover part.

She had a way of making him feel alive, engaged, challenged. She had a way of making life feel surprising and fun.

It hadn't felt like that for a long time, not since his father had died.

So here was the thing he needed to be grateful for: the potential for love had been there. And its forces were so powerful, so all-consuming, a man could forget the lessons love had already taught him.

Jolie had done him a big favor by pulling back.

Even the abruptness—no goodbye, a text, for God's sake—was a favor. It quashed that very real temptation to go after her, to try and catch her before she boarded that plane.

But no, now Jay could be mad, instead of sad.

Sometimes it felt as if his anger was the only thing that helped him make it through the weeks ahead, as the hot summer gave way to the cooler days of September.

"Jay!" his sister, Kelly, said. "What is wrong with you? You're acting like a bear with a sore bottom."

They had met at her favorite deli, and picked up lunch.

Unfortunately, a guy had been standing outside with a guitar and an open case. His singing—if it could be called that—had reminded Jay of Anthony outside Jolie's cabin that night.

He'd thrown five bucks inside the guitar case, but suggested the troubadour might want to think about a different career path.

Was that acting like a bear with a sore bottom?

"I did the guy a favor," he told his sister. "Like Simon on that show."

"Exactly like him!" Kelly said, triumphantly. "Grumpy old men."

He could protest that he wasn't that old, but he didn't have the energy. In fact, in the last while, since the wedding, he did feel old. Disillusioned. Okay, grumpy.

They were walking together through the old neighborhood, their deli purchases in a paper bag, bringing them to share it with their mom at their old house.

They walked by the high school, and Jay had had a sharp memory of Jolie.

His life seemed to be filled with sharp—and unwanted—memories of her.

He thought, about a thousand times a day, of sending her a quick text. Casual. *How you doing? I'm sorry we didn't have a chance to say goodbye.*

But then all that anger at her leaving like that just resurfaced.

He was pretty sure *bear with a sore bottom* didn't say the half of it. Neither did *grumpy old men.*

"Is that how you treat your clients?" Jay said, determined to deflect his sister, and remove his attention from the high school in a deft two-birds-with-one-stone conversational maneuver. "Is *what is wrong with you* your lead question? I think that's what they're paying you to find out.

"I don't treat family members like clients."

"Well, they can be thankful for that. Would *bear with a sore bottom* be like an official diagnosis? Or *grumpy old men*? From *The Diagnostic and Statistical Manual of Mental Disorders*? I remember the name of the book, because I paid for it."

There. A not-so-subtle reminder that a little gratitude might be more appreciated than *this*.

"I would never diagnose a family member," Kelly said with a sniff.

"It seems to me you've called me both a workaholic and commitment-phobe."

"Those aren't diagnoses! Observations."

Kelly had invited him for lunch with their mom. He'd talked to his mom on the phone a couple of times since the wedding, and taken her out for lunch once, but hadn't been over to their old house.

The house—a museum to how things used to be—was depressing.

"If I didn't know you better, I'd say you're having problems with love."

He snorted derisively. "You know my feelings about love."

"Yes, I do. And that belief system could cause you real difficulties if you found someone you cared about."

Ha ha, little Miss Know-It-All, as it turns out, I wasn't the problem.

"You're wrong, you know," Kelly said softly. "About love. Mom wasn't destroyed by the loss of her great love."

"Oh, geez, a lecture from the twenty-four-year-old expert on all things."

"It's because she was so codependent that she can't recover."

He swore under his breath. "I thought you didn't diagnose family members."

"Do you know what codependency is?" his sister asked.

"Vaguely. The more apt question would have been, do I want to know what it is. To which the answer is—"

His sister cut him off, undeterred. "It's putting everyone else's needs ahead of your own all the time. It's knowing what they need, but not what you need. It's knowing what they like, but not what you like."

Jay remembered telling Jolie about his mom planning those game nights. She would start on Monday planning an event for Friday.

As if her whole life revolved around that.

"She just wanted to make us happy," he told his sister.

"Yes, but then Dad died, and we grew up, and she doesn't have a clue how to make herself happy. She used to paint. Did you know that?"

"No." He felt suddenly guilty at how little he

knew about the mother who had known absolutely everything about him.

"I've signed her up for some painting lessons. I'm going to tell her over lunch. I want you to back me up."

"Okay," he said, "I will."

"I wish you would remember that when you're convincing yourself about the failure of love," Kelly said softly.

"What?"

"That we had each other's backs. You and me and Mike and Jim. Look at how you stepped up for us, Jay, after Dad died. You took on all kinds of stuff that a young guy probably really wasn't equipped to deal with. But you did deal with it. You made whatever sacrifices you had to make, you did whatever it took to make sure we had education and opportunities, and most importantly, with Mom falling apart, stability. If that isn't love, I don't know what is. You showed us how to step up for each other."

He wondered about his level of self-involvement that he hadn't made note of this before. Yes, initially, he had been the one to shoulder the responsibility when his dad died.

But now his siblings stepped up for him. Consistently. Unquestioningly.

Kelly insisted on coffee or dinner with him at least once a week. His brothers were always coming up with tickets for guy activities. They all texted back and forth. It was now his siblings that arranged family activities that included his mom.

As well as his family, hadn't his friend Troy always been there for him, too? Quietly in the background, saying without ever needing to say the words, *I got your back, bro.*

The faint animosity he'd been feeling toward Kelly evaporated. It didn't have anything to do with her, anyway.

He put his arm around her shoulder and kissed the top of her head.

"You're a good person," he said, and she beamed at him.

They came around the corner, their old family home now in sight, across the street and two doors down. Both of them stopped in their tracks.

There was a landscaping truck out front. The neglected flower bed, the one between the house and the sidewalk that Jolie had remembered, was all torn up.

The weeds were out of it, and it was filled with mounds of fresh, deep dark loam. His mother was outside, in her nightgown. She rarely got dressed anymore. She was walking up and down, shaking her head in disbelief. A landscaper was on his knees, tucking plant after plant into that rich, new soil.

Even though he was no expert on flowers, he knew exactly what they were. Marigolds.

"Did you do this?" he asked Kelly. Had it been part of her plan to bring their mom back to life? Acting out of the love that he had been so certain had failed their family?

But she shook her head. "I was about to ask you the same thing."

Of course she hadn't done it. How would she know about the marigolds? They crossed the street together. Their mom saw them coming, and gestured them over.

"Did you two do this?"

They both shook their heads.

"It must have been Mike and Jim," she said.

Since Mike and Jim had the combined sensitivity of a rock, Jay doubted that. Very much. Also, there was the question of the marigolds.

"It's a miracle," his mom whispered.

'It's just flowers," he told her gruffly.

"No, no, it isn't. I asked for a sign this morning."

Oh, geez. Signs and portents. Well, if they gave hope did it matter what his mom wanted to believe?

Still, he asked her. "A sign of what?"

"That life could be good again. Even without your father." She looked at him, both guilty for entertaining such a thought, and hopeful.

CHAPTER NINETEEN

"OF COURSE LIFE is going to be good again," Jay told her. When had he started believing that, particularly in the face of his current misery over Jolie's abandonment?

He put his arm around his mother's thin shoulder and kissed her head, just as he had done with his sister a few minutes ago.

"Years ago, your father brought me a marigold that he'd rescued from somewhere. Sickly thing. I planted it and it seeded itself. This whole front garden ended up having marigolds in it."

"I remember."

"Do you?" she said, surprised.

Actually, he was not sure he had given it a thought until Jolie brought it up.

"That year I had done geraniums," his mother said, softly. "Red, white, red, white, it was all very orderly. I thought of it as my Canadian theme. That marigold did not go at all."

"Why'd you plant it, then?"

"To make him happy," his mother admitted.

"The funny thing is, it ended up making me happy, too."

Oh, this complicated, twisted, wonderful thing called family. You couldn't really capture the dynamics of all the different kinds of love—healthy and unhealthy—with labels.

He moved away from his mother and his sister.

"Hey," he said to the landscaper, who set down an armful of the bedding plants and turned to look at him. "What are you doing?"

"Planting," he said, annoyed at being interrupted to state the obvious.

"It's just that this is my mother's house, and she didn't order any flowers. My sister and I didn't, either."

The landscaper became more garrulous. "Wrong time of year, really, and hard to find marigolds that are perennials, but if the price is right miracles can be accomplished."

Miracles.

Jay looked over at his mom. "Who ordered the work?" he asked, as if he didn't know.

"Uh, I can't say. It's confidential."

Jay could say, of course, that his mother was the homeowner, and she hadn't ordered the work and had a right to know who did, but that seemed unnecessarily querulous. And might not get him to where he needed to be.

Since the man had already let it be known miracles could be accomplished for the right price, Jay took his wallet out of his pocket and practiced his superpower with two bright red Canadian fifty-dollar bills.

The guy glanced at them, took them without hesitation, and then slid them into his pocket.

"Some doctor in Italy. Weird, eh?" And then he turned back to his work.

Jay stood there, stock-still, for a moment.

Even though he'd known, it hit him hard that Jolie was thinking of him, too.

Not him, precisely, but the thing in his life that was causing him pain, how his family dynamic had changed since the death of his father. Perhaps she, like his sister, saw that as holding him back.

From love.

Did she want him to overcome that obstacle? Is that what this gift of the garden for his mom meant?

Was it a hint?

Not exactly. He saw, suddenly, precisely what it was. It was an invitation. Not just to participate in something that had been dropped in his lap, like their accidental engagement.

But to make a choice for himself.

Choosing it was momentous.

Jolie had to know that.

But what she couldn't have known, was that

her gift to his family had arrived on the same day that his mother was pleading for a sign.

That it was okay to go on living.

That life would be good again.

It struck him that he was in the middle of an energetic force that was all intertwined, and that logic could never explain. He was right in the middle of the incredible mystery that was the interconnectedness of life.

What hope did he, a mere mortal, have of fighting such a force? Even if he wanted to?

Which he didn't.

"Hey," he said to the landscaper. "Can I get an address for the doctor in Italy?"

"Oh—" the landscaper looked suddenly shifty "—that's not really my department."

But it turned out, for a price, it could be.

Jolie sat on her terrace and breathed in deeply. She had changed clothes after work, into the slip dress from the wedding. It had turned out it may not have been the perfect bridesmaid dress, but it was the perfect loungewear for hot Italian evenings, particularly now since she had removed the stitched-in second slip.

She loved evenings. Her view and this terrace made up for the tininess of her apartment.

It was breathtaking, looking over the clay-tiled rooves of Rome to the Vatican in the distance.

The setting sun was painting the roof of the Basilica of Saint Peter in shades of gold.

She was appreciative of the fact she could once again end her days with a glass of wine, since she was definitely not pregnant.

She took a sip of the wine, and watched a butterfly toy with the edges of the bright begonias that spilled out of her window boxes. She felt, astonishingly, as if she could hear the air under its wings.

She'd had this amazing feeling since returning from Canada.

Not of being diminished by her time with Jay.

But rather, made alive by it, as if his kisses trailing fire down her heated skin had called sleeping senses to life. She saw things differently and deeply, she heard sounds she had never heard before, the scent of a single flower could captivate her whole body.

As she watched the butterfly, a crisp knock came on her door. It was too hot to cook, so she had ordered dinner from her favorite trattoria around the corner. It was already paid for by credit card. The delivery service could leave it, so she didn't miss the setting of the sun.

The knock came again.

Firmer.

At least she was one hundred percent certain it wasn't Anthony. He had contacted her, via new phone number since his old one was blocked, shortly after her return to announce, a trifle smugly, that he'd moved on.

There'd been a picture attached to the text.

Jolie was pretty sure that it was the same woman she'd seen him sharing *their* spaghetti and meatballs ice cream with.

Anthony asked after her engagement, but she hadn't answered, just blocked his new number. There had been no sense of vindication in blocking that number, just a sense of a clean cut, a chapter closed.

The knocking came again, even firmer, and with a resigned sigh she set down her wineglass and pushed back her chair. The woman she'd been a week ago probably would have gone and put a light wrap over her practically transparent dress, but the new her did not care what people thought.

If they thought she was sexy, good. Her time with Jay had taught her that. She *was* sexy. She liked being sexy. It was part of embracing being a woman to acknowledge that about yourself.

She went through her tiny apartment to the door. Her building was three hundred years old, well before peepholes in doors had been a thing.

Not worried it would be Anthony and expecting a question about her credit card, she pulled it open.

Nothing could have prepared her for the shock of Jay standing there.

Her newly attuned senses were flooded. Even though he must have been traveling, he smelled wonderful.

Of course, private jets would do that, keep the travails of travel to a minimum, she told herself, trying to keep some semblance of a barrier in place.

He was dressed in a casual suit, which also was not travel rumpled. She'd never seen him in a suit before. It was beautifully cut to skim his sleek masculinity. It hinted at his power, rather than bragging about it.

It was also mouthwateringly sexy.

At least as sexy as the little dress she had on.

But there was also no mistaking, not just in the cut of his clothes, but in the way he held himself, that the man was a billionaire, just as they were portrayed on the covers of books and magazines.

He had sunglasses on. They shielded his eyes and gave him a celebrity quality. She could see her reflection in them.

She tucked a stray curl behind her ear. She needn't have bothered. It leaped right back to where it had been before.

"Hi," he said, casually.

His hair was longer than when she had first seen him getting out of his car at Hidden Valley all those months ago. But then, as now, the setting sun was adding threads of gold to the light brown strands.

He was also sporting a faintly roguish look, whiskers darkening the perfect, chiseled planes of his cheeks and chin.

"Hi?" she said, trying to hide the hard pounding of her heart. Her attuned senses were flooded with him, and it made it hard to resist the desire to fling herself at him *again*. Had she learned nothing at all from her past flingings?

Jolie folded her arms in front of herself, over the transparency of the dress. It was a small gesture against the swamping of her defenses.

"Hi," she said, "as in you were just in the neighborhood and thought you'd pop by?"

"Something like that. Don't look at me as if I'm a stalker to add to your collection of men you've spurned."

"*Spurned* seems a little strong."

He lifted the sunglasses. Oh, those eyes! A shade of green that should be criminal, since it could be used as a weapon against a weakening heart.

Too easy to remember how the color of those eyes had darkened with passion each time Jay had lowered his head to kiss her.

Actually, it seemed as if maybe they were darkening a shade now, as he took in the dress.

"Does it?" he asked, quietly.

"Does what?" she stammered, getting lost in the look in his eyes, losing the conversational thread completely.

"Does *spurned* seem like too strong an expression for what you did to me?"

"Yes!"

It was sweltering, the day's heat trapped up against her front door. Reluctantly, she stepped back, let Jay in, shut the door behind him.

His presence made her cozy space seem even tinier. She knew, no matter what happened, he would always be here now, his presence leaving an imprint.

"I like this," he said.

The man who could have and buy anything liked her apartment?

Big deal.

She wondered if he'd like the bedroom. That was the problem with letting Jay in, particularly since her senses had gone wild.

"I'm trying to understand why you left me the way you did," he said. She wanted to close her eyes and listen. Not to the words. To the tone. The faint rasp.

"Just kind of mid-dance," he continued. "No goodbye."

"Come out to the deck," she said. "We'll catch

the last of the sun going down. You can see Saint Peter's from there."

So first she'd invited him in. And now they were going to the deck. And then she'd pour him a glass of wine. In fact, she grabbed a wineglass off an open shelf as they passed through her apartment, the kitchen and the living room all sharing a space.

He was edging into her life, one inch at a time.

And she was allowing it.

If the butterflies in her stomach were any indication, she was *loving* it.

"I sent a text," she said, pouring him a glass of wine. He took off the suit jacket and draped it over the back of his chair, then sat down.

He lifted an eyebrow at her as he lifted the wineglass to his lips. "Right," he said, "a text."

"Okay, maybe I should have done that differently, but you're not exactly without sin, either."

Sin.

She could think of a few she wished they were committing right this second!

CHAPTER TWENTY

"Sin," Jay said, with a certain amount of wicked relish. "That sounds like something from our Catholic high school."

"You are in Rome. Let he who is without sin…"

"You're keeping me in suspense. What's my sin?"

His sin? So many of them. Where to begin? Bringing out the passionate side in her, making the entire world with all its rules disappear when she was in his arms, making her believe in something she had sworn off…

"You forgot to tell me a few things about yourself," Jolie informed him.

"Such as?"

"Oh, you know, the billionaire part."

"Okay, that's a first. A woman saying that as if it's a bad thing."

"It's not the billionaire part, exactly, that's the bad thing. It's you not telling me."

"You left the wedding that night because you thought I was a billionaire?" he said skeptically.

"Aren't you?"

"Having a billion dollars in sales is not the same as being a billionaire."

"Now you're splitting hairs."

"I would have thought success would make me more attractive, not less." He pushed his hair back off his forehead. It flopped back down as if he hadn't touched it at all.

"Jolie, I didn't tell you because I wanted, just for a while, for it to be the same as it was before I achieved success. Like it was in high school, where people just liked me for me."

"You're deluded. They liked you because you were the captain of the football tcam. And you were good-looking. And had a great ass."

"People are that superficial?" he asked, with mock horror.

"Yes."

"The point I'm trying to make is that when you first achieve success, it's not what you think it's going to be. It's lonely. You can't take people at face value anymore. It's exhausting trying to sort out if someone's interested in you for you, or if their interest is about what you can do for them."

He was actually making her feel sorry for him. That was ridiculous!

"I saw the pictures of you at home with some of the world's most well-known celebrities," Jolie said firmly. "You didn't look exhausted."

"That's what I'm trying to tell you. When it first all hits, it feels like you need a new world. So you gravitate to people who have as much as you.

"Then you find out sometimes those people—like Sophie—have the limelight on them all the time. They're in a cage that they can't get out of. They hate the attention. They love the attention. Often, they need the attention for their careers. Lots of them regard any kind of publicity as good publicity.

"So, yes, I stuck my toes in the waters of that world. I found I couldn't live with that kind of scrutiny. If you stubbed your toe and had a scowl on your face, the day's headline was that you'd had a big fight with your lover.

"The thing is, if you get too deep into that world, you can't get back out. Things are never going to be normal for you again.

"And maybe because that's what I grew up with, that's what I crave. Normal. I had to make choices, and so I've chosen a small inner circle of people I can trust.

"My family, my sister and brothers. Old friends. No one keeps me down-to-earth quite like Troy, saying *Oh, get over yourself, you still suck at a pickup game of basketball.*

"When we first met again, it was so apparent to me that you didn't know about my success, I wanted you to be like that, too. I would have told you sooner or later, but I just wanted to be an average guy for a while. What would have changed if I would have told you?"

Jolie sighed. "Have you ever heard the expression, *punching above your weight*?"

"Sure. Hasn't everybody?"

"It doesn't translate to Italian. I heard Jack and Jill talking. That's what they said about me and you."

"Punching above your weight doesn't have to mean you're in the wrong class. It can mean you have enough confidence in yourself to try anything."

Why did he always, always seem to see her in a different light than the one she saw herself in?

"That's not how they said it," she said tightly.

"And that's why you left? Without even saying goodbye?"

She nodded, tightly.

"I don't believe that's true. Not that they didn't say it, but that anything those two witches said would affect how you felt about me."

"I looked you up online after I overheard them. The plane. Hobnobbing with the rich and famous. It was obvious to me it was true. I was punching way above my weight."

He stared at her, and then he reached across the table and took her hand in his. He squeezed.

"What's really going on, Jolie?" he asked, his voice soft. "Because after that, you planted marigolds for my mom?"

"How did you find out that was me?"

"Oh, you know, that billionaire secret weapon. My superpower."

"What's your superpower?" she asked.

"Throw some money at it."

She looked at his lips. She couldn't stop herself. She said, "That's not your superpower."

He smiled at her. "Now," he said with satisfaction, "we're getting somewhere."

She sighed. What was really going on? With his hand in hers, she felt safe telling him the full truth.

"I was embarrassed, Jay. I set up the fake engagement. And then I seduced you. I was the aggressor. And, all that time, I had no idea how far out of my league you were."

He cocked his head. "There's still something you're not telling me."

It was terrifying to be seen like this.

Terrifying, and as if she had been waiting her whole life for it at the same time.

"Sabrina told me she was pregnant."

His brow lowered. "Holy. Does Troy know?"

"I nearly got slapped for asking that."

"Well, he didn't want to have kids yet."

"So I knew that, and I was considering the

super yucky possibility she'd trapped him. Using the same trap my mom used on my dad."

"Oh, Jolie," he said, "I'm sad that's how your parents got together and even sadder that you knew. Kids should not know stuff like that."

"Sabrina got it thrown in her face every time they had an argument."

"That explains a few things about Sabrina," he said.

"I know."

"As gut-wrenching as all this is, what does it all have to do with us?" he asked.

Complete confession time. They were in the Catholic capital of the world, after all.

"In the throes of passion, I didn't think about birth control," she admitted.

He went very still. "That's not totally on you. I must have been carried away myself. I can't believe it never once occurred to me." And then, quietly, "Are you?"

"No."

Did he actually look faintly disappointed?

"No, Jay, I'm not. But if I had been, wouldn't it have looked as if I set a trap for the billionaire?"

"Pretty sure I just saw that title on a book at a kiosk at the airport."

She smacked him on the shoulder. She'd missed doing that. From the look on his face, he might have missed it, too. "I don't think you've been in the public spaces in an airport for quite some time."

"Okay, I saw it at my sister's house, but she'd kill me for outing her for reading *Setting a Trap for the Billionaire*."

"You did not see a book with that title.

"Okay, maybe not *exactly* that title, but I'm still going to summarize that plot, through your point of view, which is romance writer talk."

"How would you know?"

He wagged wicked eyebrows at her. "I know lots of things. So, to summarize, you seduced me, and then thought you might be pregnant. And didn't want it to seem like you were trying to snag yourself a billionaire, so you left without saying goodbye."

"Yes, that sums it up."

"Except for the marigolds."

She was silent for a moment. Then she said, "I just wanted your mom to know somehow, that when love leaves you, maybe it comes back in a different way."

"I don't think that's all it was, Jolie."

The look on his face made her heart go very still.

"I think it was an invitation," he told her softly.

"For what?" she squeaked

"You were right. You set up the engagement. And then you seduced me." He paused.

"But those marigolds sent me a message. You hadn't left me. You certainly hadn't left me because I was a billionaire.

"You did what a woman with dignity and self-respect—a woman who knows her own worth—would do. You invited me. You said, *You want me? We have a future? It's your turn. You make the move. You be the leader. You prove yourself worthy of me.* And that's why I traveled around the world. To accept your invitation. To make my move."

CHAPTER TWENTY-ONE

JOLIE LET THAT sink in, stunned.

Jay Fletcher had traveled halfway around the world to make a move on her, to see if they had a future together.

To see if *he* was worthy of *her*.

"So, where should we start?" he asked her.

She knew exactly where to start. She was out of her chair in a flash, on his side of the table, in his lap, twining her arms around his neck.

Kissing him.

"No," Jay said firmly, "not this time."

"I know what I want," she said, nuzzling his lips, feeling like a person dying of thirst who had just found water—

That line had worked so well last time. This time, Jay gently scooted out from under her. She found herself sitting in the chair alone, gazing up at him.

"Jolie," he said firmly. "I'm taking the lead this time."

"What does that mean?" she said, and heard a touch of sulkiness in her voice.

"I knew exactly who you were when you were sixteen," he said softly. "Do you remember what I said to you that night?"

"Almost word for word," she said, and not happily.

"I said," he reminded her softly, "that you weren't a fling kind of girl, that I could see forever in your eyes. You still aren't that kind of girl. Woman. I still see the same thing in your eyes that I always saw. A longing for happily-ever-after. You're the forever kind. We have to find out if I am, too."

"How?" she stammered. Jay was talking about him and her happily-ever-after. *Forever?*

Sometimes you did not allow yourself to admit how badly you wanted something.

And then someone spoke it out loud, and with their word breathed life and hope into your secret dream.

"I'm going to court you, in an old-fashioned way. It means I'm going to treat you with complete honor and respect, just like I did the night of the senior prom."

"Well," she said, and then to hide the fact it felt like she might be going into a good old-fashioned swoon, "that sounds perfectly dull."

"I'm going to woo you and romance you."

"It's getting a little better," she decided. "But we're going to kiss, right?"

He tilted his head, considering. "Occasionally," he decided, and then, dead serious, "Jolie, I'm going to be the man my father raised me to be."

Even though she just wanted to drag him into the bedroom and seduce him all over again, she was also intrigued by the relationship plan he was outlining.

Honored by it.

"So," he said, "if a billionaire dropped by unexpectedly to see you in Rome, where would you suggest going out for dinner?"

"I've ordered dinner. It should be here any minute."

"If you hadn't ordered dinner, where?"

"There's a place I walk by on my way to work at the Colosseum. It's pretty famous for its food and ambience. I've always wanted to go there. It probably takes months to get reservations, though."

"Ah," he said, "billionaire superpower number two. A personal assistant named Arnold. If he can't do it, it can't be done."

And so it began, with an exquisite candlelight dinner at one of Rome's most exclusive restaurants. She was pretty sure that she caught a glimpse of Al Pacino.

When they got home the dinner she had ordered was waiting on the steps, and they ate that, too!

And that's how it unfolded.

Jay was a perfect gentleman. He spoiled her with surprise weekend drop-ins. He picked her up in his private plane and they explored Paris together. He sent the plane to get her so she could join him when he had business in New York. They explored that city as the leaves began to fall.

They toured museums and sampled wine and had box seats for sporting events and concerts.

As fall turned to winter, they went heli-skiing in the Canadian Rockies, and skating on Ottawa's Rideau Canal.

Jolie loved the glitz and glamour! Of course she did. And yet what she came to love best of all were the unexpected moments that became so special because their very simplicity allowed her to see how Jay shone in the world.

One of her favorite moments was a stop for a hamburger at a little hole-in-the-wall run by a couple who had been married for forty-five years.

Or when they walked through a park and stopping to watch a little boy and his sister making ships out of leaves and sailing them across puddles.

Her favorite things became not five-star restaurants and jaunts to exotic places in the private jet, but pizza, with hand-stretched crust like Nonna had taught her, and a movie at home.

His hand in hers on a chilly day.

The way his eyes lit up every single time he saw her.

The tenderness in his voice when he spoke to her.

The biggest surprise of all was how much she started to love going back to Toronto. In fact, it began to squeeze out their explorations of other places in the world.

When Jolie came home, she and Jay would hang out with Sabrina and Troy, watching her sister's belly grow. It was delightful to witness how excited Troy was about becoming a dad.

For the first time in her life, Jolie enjoyed being around her parents. She wasn't sure if Jay's billionaire status put them on their best behavior, but there seemed to be new rules between them.

If she was not mistaken, her mother was not begging anyone to love her anymore.

Once, when they were together, that song came on.

"My namesake," Jolie said wryly.

Her mother looked puzzled. "What? This song? You were named after my favorite auntie. She died right before you were born."

And so this, too, was a lesson in family.

What you thought about your family was one

part truth, and one part myth, and all the other parts were perception.

She loved meeting Jay's mom. She radiated the sweetness of a person who gave their heart completely.

And she gave it completely to Jolie.

She talked Jolie and Jay into taking a painting class with her.

"Do you think the paint is edible?" Jay asked Jolie in an undertone, midclass, obviously getting bored.

"No, it's not edible!" she told him, but giggled, remembering the avocado mask. Was there anything in the world quite as nice as a man who would go to great lengths to make you giggle?

He ate a blob of the paint.

Just as his mother looked their way, too. His mom sighed with a pretense of long-suffering.

"He's always been like that," she told Jolie, and then to Jay's embarrassment regaled the whole art class with stories of things he had done when he was young.

Jay and Jolie spent rowdy nights watching baseball games in sports bars with his brothers. She adored his sister, Kelly, and the silliness of the game events that she held at her small apartment on Friday nights.

She loved being witness to how those people that Jay had chosen for his inner circle loved him.

And respected him.

Through it all, no matter how she tried to tempt him, and oh, she did, Jay would not break.

Hard no to hanky-panky, he'd remind her, when she'd plant a kiss on his neck, or sneak one onto his lips.

"I've been thinking about Christmas," he told her one night on the phone. "You said, growing up, it was the worst time for you."

Her heart just filled with tenderness that he always remembered these things.

"So, I thought it's time to make new memories. I want us to have the most spectacular first Christmas together. I've narrowed it down to two places. Rovaniemi, in the Lapland of Finland or Bath, in England. They both would be really unique—"

"Jay, I never thought you would hear these words from me, but I want to spend Christmas at home."

"Home. Rome?"

When had that happened? Rome didn't feel like home so much anymore. She felt like she belonged other places, now, too.

"I just can't imagine not being around your mom at Christmas. Not seeing Kelly and Mike and Jim."

He groaned. "Kelly likes to play *all* those horrible games on Christmas Eve."

"Perfect. And how could we not have Christmas with Sabrina and Troy and my mom and dad? You know, with all its potential for disaster, maybe we could look at getting everyone together."

"One big happy family?" he said skeptically.

"Something like that," she said happily.

Here's what Jay did not like about her plan. He had an engagement ring for Jolie. It had been burning a hole in his pocket for months, while he tried to figure out exactly the right time and the right words.

It had been fun romancing her.

He felt as if he'd gotten to know her and her family, but also himself and his family so much better through the process.

But the no hanky-panky thing was becoming impossible.

A man's honor could only carry him so far.

His was going to carry him and Jolie straight to the altar. After that, he planned to make up for lost time.

Finally, he had decided, Christmas would be the best time to propose even if she had said no to Finland and Bath, both with much higher potential for romance than Toronto.

He wanted it to be Christmas because he remembered her saying it was the worst time of all for her.

And he wanted to start changing that.

With a Christmas proposal.

And then once he'd proposed—once it was official that they were going to be man and wife—if they were in Toronto, he might as well use that. He'd planned prosecco and his king-size bed and a celebration she would never forget. He planned to end their courtship with the complete seduction of Jolie.

An evening with family?

Sheesh.

Could nothing ever go according to plan?

CHAPTER TWENTY-TWO

"IS EVERYTHING OKAY?" Jolie asked Jay.

"Oh, sure." *Hunky-dory*, he thought to himself. Her plane had been late, they were in the middle of a bloody snowstorm, his sister was having both of their families over for Christmas Eve, and he had to figure out how to get that ring on Jolie's finger.

Tonight.

His mother and Jolie's father were planning the traditional *la vigilia* feast. No turkey for them. The last time he'd spoken to his mother, they were planning seven courses of seafood, since meat was a no-no.

While it was good to see his mom having enthusiasm for life again, where in the seven courses did he fit in his proposal?

Certainly he had to get it in before his sister started her infernal games, and then they were all herded off to midnight mass.

He'd confided in Troy because it seemed to

him maybe Troy knew a thing or two about proposals, having done it twice.

It was Troy who had suggested after dinner would be nice. It was rare for the whole family to get together, but they would be on Christmas Eve, so why not do it then?

Troy even suggested they could hide the ring in a Christmas firecracker thing that would be at each place setting.

Now that they were almost at Kelly's house, Jay could feel his feet getting cold. Did he really want to propose publicly? Did he get down on his knee in front of everyone? According to Troy, nothing would say commitment quite like that.

What if she said no?

For God's sake, she wasn't saying no. He glanced over at her. She looked back at him. There it was in her eyes. Forever.

He'd prepared his bedroom before he'd gone to the airport. Strawberries dipped in chocolate, prosecco on ice, new, crisp sheets. In the interest of his old-fashioned honor, he'd never let her stay at his place.

She stayed at her parents when she came here. What if she wanted to go there after midnight mass?

She wouldn't want to go there. They'd be newly engaged. It wasn't like she was six and had to be at their house so Santa could find her.

"Are you sure you're okay?" she asked.

"I said I was okay!"

Maybe he should hold off on the proposal? Until they were alone? That would be more romantic. When the heck were they ever going to be alone?

That was it. He wasn't proposing in front of both their families. He slipped into a parking spot in front of his sister's row house.

They were the last ones there. How had his sister's been picked? It was way too small. Oh, he'd gone along with that because he hadn't wanted them all at his place, when he was getting his own private celebration ready.

Troy gave him the secret handshake and a wink when they came in the door. Jolie, his wife-to-be, was swallowed up by both families who hadn't seen her for a while.

Geez, there was her sister. Sabrina looked as big as a house. He had to work at not saying it. Hadn't Troy said she had a month left?

"Sabrina," he said, "you're, ah, glowing."

There was too much noise and too many people, and his soon-to-be father-in-law and his mom were shouting in Italian in the kitchen. The smoke detector started wailing and his sister got under it with a dish towel, and waved with what appeared to be long practice until the smoke detector burped and quit.

This was not going to work.

He saw Troy laying down the firecrackers beside each plate. With the big wink at him as he set down a yellow one beside Jolie's place.

"Jolie," Troy yelled, "you sit here."

Jay scowled at him. Did he have to be so obvious? He felt like he couldn't breathe. He didn't think he could do this.

No, he hadn't thought it through.

A private moment, a nice restaurant, just her and him.

He reached over and slid her firecracker away from her plate and put it in his pocket. Troy raised his eyebrows and mouthed, *Chicken.*

Well, so be it.

Troy good-naturedly took another firecracker from the box and threw it at him. He set it in front of Jolie's plate.

But as it turned out, no one opened those firecrackers.

Because when Troy pulled back the chair for Sabrina, she suddenly clutched her stomach and cried out.

There was a sound like a balloon full of water hitting the floor. And then, as if it hadn't been chaotic enough, all hell really broke loose.

He found himself in the back seat of Troy's car with Sabrina's head on his lap and her terrified eyes glued to his face. Every now and then a whimper of pain would escape her.

Selfishly, he was glad he hadn't proposed. A stupid rhyme went through his head.

First comes love,
Then comes marriage,
Then comes Jolie pushing the baby carriage.

Only it wasn't Jolie, it was Sabrina, but did a man seriously ask this kind of pain of a woman if he loved her?

Troy drove. Jolie rode shotgun.

A whole convoy came behind them.

He said anything that came into his head. "You're doing great. Everything will be okay. Troy's a super driver. Hang in there. Five more minutes. We're almost there."

And then they were at the hospital in the driveway reserved for emergencies. Troy screeched to a halt.

"I can't move," Sabrina whispered.

Jay catapulted out of the car and ran around and over to the other passenger door. He flung it open. If he was not mistaken that was a baby's head. He rammed himself into the back seat.

And then, suddenly, he was holding a very slippery, very bloody baby, trying to protect its fragile body from the snow. For a terrifying moment, he thought the baby, a boy, was dead.

But then it gave an outraged cry, and squirmed in his hands.

And then he was being pushed out of the way, and the baby was taken from him, and there was a stretcher and cops—where had they come from—and nurses and people yelling in Italian.

And then that great wave of noise and chaos moved away from him and it was blessedly quiet.

He sank down on the curb. Alone.

Except that Jolie came and sat on that cold wet curb beside him. And laid her head on his shoulder.

He realized he was crying.

And so was she.

And then she said, "Best Christmas Eve ever."

And he took the crumpled firecracker out of his pocket and gave it to her. There was no way he was going home alone after this.

"I'm sorry," he said. "Under the circumstances it's the best that I can do."

She pulled both ends, and there was a little clicking sound, because of course the firecrackers never worked, but it ripped open nicely and her ring had the decency not to fall out and fall down the gutter.

She took the ring and put it on her finger.

And then laid her head back on his shoulder.

"Yes," she said. "A million times yes."

EPILOGUE

JAY COULD FEEL his eyes smarting as Jolie walked toward him.

She was wearing the most simple wedding gown he had ever seen. But it did exactly what those dresses should always do, but hardly ever did.

The simplicity of the dress allowed the bride to shine through.

Everything that she had become in the last few months was there: her confidence, her belief in herself, her generosity in love.

But it wasn't any of that that was making his eyes smart.

It was what she carried.

Instead of a bouquet, she had her hands cupped around a single bedraggled marigold in a plastic container.

To Jay, it looked like the most beautiful flower in the entire world. Love was exactly like that flower. If you nursed it, it would come back, stronger and better than it had ever been before. But more than that, when you planted it, it spread.

Even when the original died out, as of course it eventually would, it left its mark on the world.

That's what his mother and father's great love had done. It had left its mark on the world. It had nourished him, and his brothers and sister, given them strength, and ultimately the ability to see that love made the world better and it made people better.

It had given him the ability to help heal someone—Jolie—who had not experienced such love in her life. It had given him the gift of seeing her come to believe.

That love could be strong and true, pure and nourishing.

Eventually the gift his mother and father's great love had given him—that he had lost sight of for a while, that he had turned his back on for a while—would give again. To his children and maybe someday grandchildren and great-grandchildren.

That's what love did.

When everything else had faded away, it remained.

And it went on and on and on.

Forever.

He saw that in Jolie's eyes as she took her place in front of him at the altar. He saw there, what he had seen since she was sixteen.

Forever looked like babies taking first steps and it looked like new puppies on wobbly legs.

It looked like gardens full of marigolds.

It looked like the old ones flying away from this earth, and the sorrow of saying goodbye divided in half by love.

It looked like unexpected challenges and heartbreaking choices and losses that were every bit as much of this amazing dance as the joys were.

Love did not protect you from any of that.

Love, that thing he thought he'd said no to, had not accepted his refusal.

He listened as Jolie said her vows, her voice so strong and so sure, her forever eyes on him.

It was not part of what they had rehearsed.

Not even close.

But when her voice fell away, after she had said "I do," he leaned his forehead on hers, and he said, "Mrs. Fletcher, is that your final answer?"

* * * * *

HARLEQUIN
Reader Service

Enjoyed your book?

Try the perfect subscription for Romance readers and get more great books like this delivered right to your door.

See why over 10+ million readers have tried Harlequin Reader Service.

Start with a Free Welcome Collection with free books and a gift—valued over $20.

Choose any series in print or ebook. See website for details and order today:

TryReaderService.com/subscriptions